Country Secrets

A Bearman Story

E. A. Maynard

DEDICATION

I have been lucky enough to know some great people. Some of them are missed and thought about often. This book helps me remember them as their spirit has come to the pages in this book. My step-dad Paul Rumschlag, had a bigger-than-life personality who I will always remember.

My friend and a greatly missed confidant, Scott Byrd, had a personality and wit that lent to the creation and character of Scott Bearman. These great men will live forever through the memories of everyone who were blessed to know them. They will always be a part of my life and so many others.

CONTENTS

ACKNOWLEDGMENTS

There has been a lot of work and time put into this fictional book. This being my first book, has taken more time than expected from when I originally started this project. With the support of my family and close friends, every challenge to get here has been achieved. I am thankful to them for that and all they did to help me survive my crazy life.

In the process, I was lucky to have found Rob Hillier, who created Sylexiad Font and can be found at Sylexiad.com. Mr. Rob Hillier has graciously allowed me to use his font. The Sylexiad font is a selection of fonts for adult dyslexic readers. I have found his font to be very helpful to me in my writing.

Thank you Mr. Rob Hillier.

Chapter One

Some of my stories may seem farfetched. So, I ask you to remember two things as I tell you about this part of my life. First, I did not plan on any of this and the second is that I did what I had to.

As I tell you this story, I will tell you everything as best as I can remember it, but forgive me if I forgot something. There is one more fact to keep in mind. We were young and fully believed we were above the law. We were trying to make as much money as we could and enjoy our lives. I did what I did because I did not know what other options I had. I am not trying to make anyone look better or worse for what happened; just telling this story from my life.

It is easy for a good person to make bad choices as one small choice leads to the next small choice. After a while, you will look back and wonder how you got to where you are. I know most people don't make the same choices I had and I accept that.

There is no need to start on day one. After two years of growing my business of selling drugs and other things, I had everything going my way. I ran a small business that was being overseen by a guy named John out of New York City. He was more dangerous than anyone I knew and his guys taught me the tricks of running my business. This brings us to the summer after graduation. I was no longer selling, but had a group of kids doing it for me. That is just a part of who I was.

The night before everything started to fall apart was one of my greatest memories. I was with three guys who were close to me and I considered them to be my friends. We were sitting under a bridge that had a large landing where we kept some lawn chairs. It was a humid night, but being a summer night in nineteen-ninety eight, I didn't expect anything else. We had just graduated and were happy that we didn't have to deal with school anymore.

This brings us to where we are now in the story. My friends were with me under this bridge enjoying a nice early Ohio summer night and each person had a bottle of their favorite whiskey. I was in a good mood, so I brought them to give as gifts to my friends. We sat out of sight and were joking around, as we were only there to hang out before a party that was going on.

Adam Byrd, who I called Duke, was a tanned, athletic guy with black hair who loved to wear his cargo shorts, opened a bottle of Jack Daniel and took a swig. Out of nowhere, Duke told everyone that he was going to leave the small town life and see the world. Duke told us about meeting people from areas that he saw in pictures and enjoy women that will bring both joy & pain. I loved when he said that he would wake up on a beach looking at the moon and holding a woman he just met that day. This made me chuckle as everyone in a small town likes to talk about leaving, but most don't go anywhere. Duke was the biggest dreamer of the group but had the biggest heart of our group too. Duke was the guy you love to know and he would give the shirt off his back for a friend.

That is when Jon Rigg, aka Riggs, held his bottle of vodka looking at it. He had a blank look on his face and was thinking about what he wanted for the future. He was a tall skinny brown haired guy that liked to be the life of the party. Riggs tilted the bottle up and told us his hopes for his future. Riggs said that he would find a woman as crazy as himself, and then move to Florida for a life of fun in the sun. Riggs continued to talk of a house on the beach and the parties he would have. After telling us what his future has in store for him, he sat back and went back to his private thoughts. Riggs had a habit of getting lost in his own thoughts. He tends to be full of dreams, just lacked the drive to do anything. Riggs was a good guy, but I personally expected him to die from his liver or kidney giving out. He had a bad drinking issue back then.

So that brings me to Dan. Dan had just taken another large swig out of his Jim Beam bottle when he started to laugh. "You guys have it all wrong. The best thing is to own your own business and be the one to make all the rules. "Bearman, you know what I am talking about." Dan kept telling us of how rich he planned to be and what his current business idea was. I found humor in some of his "businesses" that he tried to start. He was simply always looking for an angle to make money. Dan just had an issue of expecting others to do the work for him and make him money. He never thought about doing the work himself.

Dan and I were both good looking guys with dark hair and complexions that resembled a year-round tan. He had a scar from his eye to his ear I gave him when we first met. It was not easy for us to get past the fight we had on our first meeting. Dan joined our group with Riggs and over time, Dan and I did not trust each other, but were friends.

Now it comes to me. My name is Scott Bearman and I tend to go by my last name. I was a relaxed guy that was full of myself and thought I would run everything from behind the curtain. When it was my turn to say what I had planned, I told them I wanted a simple life. The type of life I wanted was not to be known by most people as I liked my privacy. I explained why I thought being behind the scene held the real money and power. That is when I pulled out a Marlboro Red and my Zippo lighter.

We were a good group that mostly came together because of Duke. Duke was a friend to everyone and the four of us hung out the most together. I try not to talk too much because Duke was the only one I really trusted, but I had fun when the four of us got together. We were not the popular kids in our school, but we were liked by almost all the cliques.

After I lit up my cigarette, Riggs jumped up and yelled that it's time for the barn party we were already late for. This party was a special one for me. I was dating a girl named Rose for over a year. Rose and I were making plans for the years to come. At this party I had a surprise for Rose that I planned to change everything for us. It seemed as if we had all forgotten about the party, but we did not want to put the caps on our bottles and get on the road. I forgot who set up that party, but I remember lots of people were planning to come.

Riggs climbed into Dan's car and then drove off to the party. Duke and I got into my truck, and he asked me what I really thought my future held. As I pulled my truck on the road, I did not say anything. After a mile, I told Duke that my life may not have the world travels like him, partying like Riggs, or the wealth that Dan believes he will make. My life will be filled with something more than all those things combined. I will have the storybook life of love, passion, and maybe a kid. Now there were only two people who I would talk to about these things to. Duke and Rose were close enough to me, I would tell them anything they asked me. I would never hide anything if they asked. I believed they also knew not to ask certain questions.

We reached a rundown barn that was about 10 minutes outside of my hometown. This was an old barn hidden away down a quarter mile driveway in the woods. Once you got into the wooded area, it opened up. The party was already well on its way. People were dancing and talking to each other. There was music blasting from a truck with a bed full of speakers next to a large bonfire, and three kegs. As Duke and I got out of my truck, our girlfriend's came up to us with a beer in hand and a big kiss on their lips. Oh and let me tell you that the kiss I got could be blamed for some of the polar ice melting. To be totally truthful, most of Rose's kisses would make me feel like I could fly to the moon and back.

Duke went off with his girlfriend Jenny and met up with Riggs and Dan. Rose and I sat on the bed of my truck. She asked why we weren't going to the party, but for the first time in my life, fear had filled me to the point I couldn't think straight. So, of course, Rose laughed at me and told me to either tell her what is on my mind or we should get to the party.

I got up and went into my truck to grab a box out of the center console and returned to where she sat, and I kissed her. While she sat on my tailgate, I got into my truck bed and sat behind her. I put her between my legs and pulled her close to me. Rose began to giggle asking what I was doing. That is when I pulled out a ring and put it in her hand. Then leaned close to her and whispered in her ear, "Will you agree to grow old with me?" The next thing I knew, she had turned around and tackled me so fast that I hit my head on the bed of the truck. She kissed me and repeatedly said yes before running off to tell her friends.

I couldn't see straight as I sat back up. Once I was able to focus my eyes, Duke, Riggs, and Dan were walking my way. I picked up what was left of the beer Rose brought and rubbed the back of my head. My friends were smiling and laughing at me as they walked closer and Rose ran by them. Dan handed me a new beer and asked if hitting my head knocked any sense into me. We all laughed and began giving each other a hard time. Duke gave me a light shove and we walked to join the rest of the party. As we walked, some people congratulated me and others told me I was crazy. I had no clue who most of these people were.

After two more beers and a lot of people stopping me, everyone wanted to tell me what they thought about me getting married. I finally found Rose standing in the middle of a group of other girls. As I walked closer to her, I overheard one girl ask Rose why she would want to marry me. This made me smile because people have been asking her why she was with me for a while. Rose saw me and she knew from the look on my face that I heard the question. Rose said loud enough that she knew I could hear, that she knows I love her and she wants to marry me and that is all she needs. Rose then walked up and gave me a big hug and kiss.

As the night ended and dawn began, the fire burned out, and most of the people there were passed out all over. I remember seeing people in beds of trucks, hoods of cars, and some were on the ground. Those of us who were still awake; drank water from a milk jug to get the beer and whiskey out of our system. The small group of us sat talking about nothing. There was one guy who to this day I don't know who he was. Riggs was with us, but he was one of the people passed out on the ground. Don't ask me why, but Riggs was asleep next to the door of his girlfriend's car, while she was sleeping in the back seat and Dan's girlfriend was sleeping in the front passenger seat.

With the sun starting to glare into my eyes, I got up to go home. After I said my goodbyes to everyone, I got into my truck and found Rose sleeping in my back seat. She wrapped herself in one of my old blankets. With a headache from a mixture of lack of sleep and drinking all night, I leaned into the back and kissed her on the check. Then I started the truck, Duke opens the passenger door and reminded me that his car was at my place. He climbed into my truck and said that Jenny had just driven off to her parent's house.

When I say that I am going to my place, I mean that I am going to an apartment I rented for two hundred a month. The truth is that even with my sweet side, I was an asshole –of –a–son at times to my mom and step–dad. I got upset and moved out; we knew it would be best if I got my own place. I knew my real dad, but he did not want much to do with me and his side of the family did not care much for me. It was OK; they wanted nothing to do with me and the only interest we shared was the family name.

Even with me being a bad son to my parents, my mom and step–dad still helped me with filling my place with furniture. I was lucky because my step–dad helped me find a place. I paid for a year's rent up front and signed the lease. Now before you ask how I paid a year's rent, you need to know that my first place was above a restaurant in the middle of nowhere and they only charged me two hundred dollars a month.

What I remember most about that day was not getting my first place. I remember as I got into my step–dad's truck, was that he gave me a pocket knife. I still carry that pocket knife with me and have it everywhere I go. He said that every man should have a knife on him or in his truck.

This brings back to the painful drive to my place. Once we arrived, Duke slid out of the truck and went up to my apartment with my key in hand. I woke Rose up or as much as I could and helped her up to my apartment, then put her in my bed. I would have loved to crawl in bed with her, but I had to get some work done and had to meet someone driving through. I got myself cleaned up and really wished that I was not going to wait for long. But as I started down the road, I knew that no matter how long I had to wait, this guy would not show up soon enough.

I waited for about an hour or so at this old hotel on route 53 off of the Ohio Turnpike. The guy showed up in a car that looked like it is old and beat up. It was the type of car you try to pass and are afraid that a rusty part would fall off. When you listen to it though, it was easy to tell it was souped up. If I was not tired and wanting to get home for a nap, I would have talked with him about his car. Instead, I handed him two bags full of money. The nice part was that the money was counterfeit. The guy pulled out three duffel bags close to being full with different kinds of drugs. When I went to get in my truck, he stopped me and handed me a cardboard box and said I had to deal with these. After a quick few words were exchanged, everything was done and we both went on our way.

This was not the first time John had done this to me. He would have a delivery of drugs and hand off a box of guns that he had to get out of his city. Normally, these were handguns that one of his guys would have used. If it was discovered, it could be used to put his guy in prison. None of us wanted that, so I would take these guns, remove the serial numbers, and then resell them to people who preferred to not let the government know they owned guns. Selling guns was an easy thing for me.

I found that I had a few talents that most would not call legal. One of these talents was printing money that was able to pass most all detection. My issue of making counterfeit money was that I would never allow my money to be spent in Ohio. I had a feeling that if the money started to spread in Ohio, it would come back on me. So, I made an agreement with a guy in New York who had operations in New York and a few other major cities. I give him two bags of money for a duffel bag of drugs. I, in turn, have some people sell the product on the street. I was not a fan of most of the types of drugs that I was selling. I realized that I didn't have to like it; I simply liked the money the people were willing to spend on those drugs. From what I understood, the drug run between Chicago and New York was a standard route. I was on the way between. This made things better for my friend in New York as his drivers needed a safe place to stay sometimes. It just happened I had a place that they could stay.

Now before I go home, I had to make a stop at an old barn out in the country where I would divide up everything. There were a few places spread around I would do this. I could not rush as I had to make sure each one of my guys got the right product. I had set up a structure where I had Mick as my second and a few others that would take care of certain areas. I would also discuss any problems that he was being told about. I had it set up that I never was around those selling any drugs at any time.

By the time I finished dividing up everything and hid it all in compartments on the bottom of my toolbox that was mounted to my truck bed. I was ready to get home and get some rest. I wanted to park my truck and get a nap before I had to meet up with some of my guys.

When I got to my apartment, I saw several cars parked in front. This was not what I wanted to see. After getting out of my truck, I walked into my apartment. Duke was the first to rush up to me. I saw Dan's girlfriend and Rigg's girlfriend sat next to Rose crying. I stood in my doorway asking for someone to explain to me what is going on and why are they there at my place. I was hoping when I got home, we would have great sex then finally sleep. I had given up hope for this when Duke started talking. Duke told me about Dan and Riggs being in the hospital from being badly beaten. I knew that Duke was not telling me everything because the girls were able to hear everything. So I asked everyone to allow me to clean up and I would handle everything I can.

You see I told Riggs, Duke, and Dan about what I was doing to a point. On occasions, they would help me out. I have also told them about a meeting I was going to miss because I did not have a good feeling about it. While I was doing other things and avoiding a meeting with the Himlee Brothers, Dan and Riggs decided to go and make a deal themselves. I don't know why Dan and Riggs felt they should go to meet with the Himlees for me. I believed that they were trying to get more into my business and wanted a piece.

What I had not told them was that Jay Himlee was very upset with a deal that I declined. He thought that I had to give him what he wanted, but when I told him he is too small for the kind of deal he wanted to do, he got upset. The Himlees ran a smaller operation and it was run by two brothers. I was able to work with the older brother and we were able to make money without stepping on each other.

The younger brother was not someone I could even talk to and he was not involved in making agreements. The main agreement I had with the brothers was that I would sell them some of my stock at my cost, as long as they stayed out of my areas. From the rumors I was told, the younger brother thought that they should become the Ohio Mob, but he was getting his product from some guy out of Detroit. What the guys did not know is that I had to deal with the real "Mob". The guys I knew from the "Mob" were not the type of people that let you do something that cuts into their business. They liked to tell me stories about people that disappeared when not doing as they were told.

Now after I canceled the meeting with these brothers, Dan and Riggs set up a meeting in my place. I would like to think that they were trying to help me or show me they could do more in my business. I wish that was what they thought. If I knew better, this would be a completely different story.

After I got out of the shower, I called Rose and Duke into the bedroom. Once they entered the bedroom, Duke closed the door behind him. As I finished getting dressed, I sat Rose down and told her about where most of my money came from. While I was explaining this all to Rose, I also was asking Duke if he knew who attacked them and why they did. You see, Duke had this way about him to get people to say things they normally would not. They just trusted him.

Duke said he would find out, and he left my place. That is when Rose started asking me questions. She wanted to know what all I have done and how long I have been doing these things and are the rumors true about me. I could only tell her "I am not sure how I got into this, but it started with doing a favor for someone and within a years' time, I had people working through me. Most people would not mess with me because of rumors. I had not done anything too violent myself yet, but I did have others do things for me." Then Rose walked out to join the others in my apartment.

I walked out of the bedroom and everyone turned to me. It was funny to me that people came to me to fix problems and assumed that I am always ready to help them. This issue was one I had to handle, but to me, it was because of who was involved. All I knew at that moment was I had a list of things to do; the first thing is to go to the hospital and see those two. I told everyone in my apartment that they could stay in my place for a bit longer. I then walked out of my own apartment and Rose ran out and got into my truck with me. The girlfriends then got into their car to follow us to the hospital.

While I drove down the road to find out more about what had happened from Dan or Riggs, Rose asked me what she should expect. Since I did not know what to say, I looked at Rose. I then said, "I hope you have nothing to worry about, but I told you about what I do so you could help keep yourself safe, I want you to be ready for whatever happens and have no surprises." I looked forward and drove.

Chapter Two

The drive seemed to be longer than what it should have been. That could be due to the questions running through my head. It also did not help that I was listening to Rose ask all kind of questions. She wanted to know more and discussed what she thought about what I had already told her. My silence was not helping her deal with finding out that I ran an illegal business, and the fact that most people would not do what I have done. I knew well enough that at that time, people spoke badly about me for what I was doing; at least those who knew. Most of those people were buying drugs from either me or the Himlee brothers.

I had a feeling that the Himlee brothers were involved with this. I had heard that the younger Himlee brother was running his mouth again. He was telling people about taking over everything and would get rid of anyone not working for him. I thought this was him being the idiot he was, since his older brother would not openly start a war with me. I made an agreement with the older Himlee brother over two years ago when we both started selling drugs. It was a simple agreement that I would not bother them as long as they stayed out of my guys' way and didn't start trouble.

As I was pulling into the hospital parking lot, I noticed three guys who did some work for me standing outside of the front doors having a smoke. I told Rose they were friends with Riggs, so that would explain why they were there. When we got out of the truck, I asked Rose to go in and find out what room Riggs and

Dan were in. She agreed and I went to talk with those guys, plus I wanted to get a smoke in before going in.

That is when I walked up to my guys and asked what they were doing here. My guy who deals with my "Area Managers" was one of the three. His name was Mick and he looked as Irish as a person could with his red hair, complexion as white as a sheet of paper, and freckles sprawling across his face. He would collect the money, give me an inventory account, and let me know of any problems I needed to address. Mick knew me well enough to know what I needed from him. You could say that Mick was my right hand man or my second-in-charge.

He told me that they came to find out what happened with Riggs & Dan being beaten up like this. I said that I would let them know when I know. Mick asked if we could meet at the house. The house is in the country that I purchased under a business name I set up and got it from a sheriff's auction. My guys and I would meet up at this place to discuss what was going on, and have parties to help our sellers feel connected to us. It tended to help the guys remain loyal to me. Everyone that came to the house would keep our rule of not telling anyone about what happens at the house, and that no one goes to the barn. The guys never thought about breaking these rules after one guy had talked to a few people about his first party. It got back to one of my Area Managers and then back to me. That is when I had a private meeting with the kid and by the end of our talk, he was hurting and a little bloody. He didn't have anything broken, but he learned his lesson. That same guy became one of our best guys.

I told Mick as I was standing there, that I had some packages for him on my truck and he could use his key to get everything. Since we have been working together, I gave him access to my truck. Sometimes he would use it if there was a lot of product that came in.

The other two guys were my Area Managers. They were two guys who Mick had collecting money and passing out product to the guys on the street and I think they knew Dan or Riggs, although I don't even remember who they said. I just remember them asking questions until Mick told them to shut up and get in his car.

After Mick sent those guys away, I walked into the hospital lobby to see Rose standing there waiting on me. I walked up to her and kissed her on the forehead, then said "You look worried. You don't have to. I will take care of it all and when you go to college next year, I will leave with you and all this drama behind." She smiled and took my hand to guide me up to Riggs and Dan's room as she already spoken to the lady at the desk.

Going up the elevator, it felt cold with the stainless steel walls. I really liked it though. There was something about the metal I liked. When I realized it, we were on the floor that the lady told us to go to. We walked down a dim hallway to the desk on that floor and the lady said that they were a few doors down towards the elevator. When we got to the room, we waited a few minutes before going into the room. I did not want to go in because I never liked to see my friends hurt. The dim hallway gave an eerie feeling like I had when my uncle died in his semi accident. We walked into the room with both of my friend's mothers sitting and talking. Both of the mothers knew me as a good heart, but a little crazy guy. They looked at me with a fake smile and sad eyes. I would have expected nothing less.

Then I heard Riggs voice in a crippling tone. I looked at him and if I did not know better, I would have thought a car hit him. It did not help to see Dan in much rougher shape and not even awake. As I looked at both of them, Riggs cleared his throat and asked if he and I could talk in private. Rose reached in my pocket and took my wallet, then offered to treat the other two to some coffee. I just smiled at her and asked her to bring me a cup back.

As the door closed with a thud, Riggs reached out and grabbed my arm. Then he told me that he and Dan went to meet the Himlee brothers to try to address the issues I had with them. He kept telling me about how Dan tried to get a bit of money out of the meeting and made an offer to the brothers. He said that the younger brother laughed. That is when their guys came over and beat the living crap out of them. Dan took most of the beating. Riggs finished with saying he heard that I would be next. He added that only the younger of the two was there.

After hearing this, I was trying to figure out what choices to make before moving forward. The problem is that I knew something had to be done quickly. With thoughts running through my head, Riggs spoke again. He told me that by the end of the summer he was joining the Marines. His mom thought he needed to straighten out and get some structure. I figured it was a good thing for him since he had a pie in the sky kind of thinking. The Marines would give him a realistic look at the world.

I was angry with the Himlee brothers, but Dan doing what he did had me just as pissed. Being filled with anger, I told Riggs that I knew Dan wanted to have some control over my business. I could only imagine that he wanted the Himlees to help. If Dan was not so underhanded, he could have come to me asking for more and I would have given him a bigger share. What made me most upset was the fact that he wanted to cut me out and betray me. The Himlees were thinking that my guys were not completely behind me and they might think they could take me out now.

Dan woke up and gave me a pain–filled look and before I was able to say anything to Dan, both mothers walked in with Rose. When they walked in they saw that I was angry. I stood in the middle of the room with my fist clinched for a short time. Without saying a word, I walked out of their hospital room and started to pace in the hallway.

Rose came out of the room and wrapped her arms around me. Draping off of me, she asked me if I can really fix this. I turned to her with so much anger in me and said that I will end this before it goes too far. I pulled Rose in close and hugged her as tight as I could. After a few minutes, I told Rose that I had things to do, and she said she would call Jenny for a ride back to my place. Then I walked down the cold hallway towards the elevator. I know now that I should have gone to talk with the older brother. I wish I would have, but that is not what happened.

After I walked out of the depressing hospital and climbed into my truck, I saw a guy walking a girl through the parking lot with half of her face bruised and an arm pulled up to her chest. I was going to drive off until I saw the guy grab the girl by the back of the neck and push her. I got out of my truck and grabbed the black crowbar I kept next to my seat. That is when I went up to the guy with my hands behind my back and the crowbar hidden.

When I reached the couple, I called the guy in a nice manner. "Excuse me, but I need your help." That is when the guy turned around and told me to kiss off (to put it nicely). I have never been a fan of rude people. Still angry over what had just happened with Riggs and Dan, and then seeing a man who beat women pushed me over my limit and I kicked his knees. This man who I never asked a name from or even cared to ask, laid on the ground holding his legs while whimpering. I don't know why, but this pissed me off more. So, I told the woman to go to the hospital and tell the police what really happened to her or this guy would not be safe from me. I also warned her that if she mentioned me, I would be back to put him in the ground.

With a few swings of the crowbar to the mans' back, I reached down and took his ID out of his pocket, then walked back to my truck. I went home and Called Duke to see what he knew. As I waited for him to pick up his phone, I started to feel the lack of sleep catching up with me. The sun was shining in my eyes and I got his answering machine, so I asked Duke to call me back or come over to talk. I must have dozed off because the phone rang and I jumped out of the chair.

It was Duke calling me back. He asked to meet me at a deli in Fostoria. He had gotten some information from one of Himlee's guys, but I did not have the energy to drive, and asked him to come to my place. He agreed and hung up his phone. I grabbed two guns that were in the box from my friend in New York and loaded them. I must have fallen back asleep because I woke to Rose walking into the apartment. Being startled, I reached for one of the guns. Luckily I realized it was Rose and let the gun drop. Rose stood there in shock as she has never even been in the same room with a gun other than hunting rifles, as far as I knew.

I went to her and held her in my arms. Rose broke down in tears and fell to the floor. She tried to talk to me through her broken tears in what sounded like a sad hiccup. I only understood a small bit of what Rose was saying. I did understand when she said that she doesn't know if she could handle all of this.

With the fear of losing her from this crap storm that has only started, we sat there in silence while I held Rose for what could've been an hour. In that time, it was as if we said more to each other and yet had never spoken a word. Then the landline rang and we both jumped.

I slowly got up off the floor and answered the phone to hear Riggs on the other end. Riggs simply said that he was being released from the hospital and would be over in two hours. I told him that he should go home and we can meet at the bridge. He said 8:00 and we hung up. I sat down on my chair and Rose came over to me. She sat on my lap, then leaned back on me as if I was some kind of lumpy pillow. Rose asked me what Riggs wanted. I said he called to tell me that he wanted to meet, and I told him Duke and I can meet tonight. After a few minutes of her staring at me, she finally told me that she wanted to be with us as we talked.

As I knew well enough, Rose was a woman that was strong-willed and does not take no as an answer too often. So I kissed her and simply asked her if she was sure that she wanted to know everything that was going to happen. That is when she walked into the kitchen and said that I need to tell Duke to bring some drinks – that is if we wanted to drink anything. She then pulled my favorite bottle of Maker's Mark bourbon from under the counter and filled my flask. She also filled a flask I had given her, but I don't remember with what.

I accepted that she needed to know what was going on. I knew that she would have to be aware of everything to be safe, but I would not let her get involved. That is why I stood up and told her I agreed and called Duke. I could not reach him and hung up the phone when I heard a knock at my door.

It turned out to be Duke anyway. Before I got a chance to answer the door, Duke walked in. He asked if Riggs had called me. Not sure why Duke was so worried, I told him that Riggs only said that he wanted to meet and I agreed to meet under the bridge. Duke said that he was told that Riggs was telling people about how Dan had some big plans and he was a big part. They did not go into details or no one paid any attention to him. No one would believe that they would have done something to hurt me, but most people are rarely what they seem. We talked for a few hours as we explained to Rose what I did and about the Himlee brothers.

I told Duke that at six, we needed to go and get him some drinks. We walked out to a humid summer evening and got in my truck. After a short time, we pulled into the corner store and I walked in as Duke sat in the truck having a smoke. I knew the guys that worked at this store, and they never checked anyone's ID, which is why I came to this specific store. What I did not know was the guy at the counter had started working for my guy Mick. I laughed when he tried to sell me some weed. That is when I sat down a case of beer and I told him no thanks. I gave him some advice and told him not to try and sell to everyone who walks past. He asked me what I knew about selling or how to go about it. The only thing I could say was I knew more than he realized. I left and walked back to my truck with two packs of cigarettes and my case of Bud Light.

It did not take long and we were back at my place. As we walked in, Rose was cooking. I slide past her to put away the beer and grab some for us to have. I figured a beer before we went would be a good idea. I also knew Duke would not say no to a cold beer. I turned towards Rose and realized that the life I'd built was in danger. I could not help to think about how it was tough to build what I had. With all that, it only took two people calling themselves my friends to put it all at risk.

Dan and Riggs who demanded revenge and would not settle for less. What Dan and Riggs did not realize was that I now knew what they were trying to do. The bad thing for me was that they were being protected under my name as a close friend of mine.

This meant that I had to do something or people would think they could do anything. Though the youngest Himlee brother most likely would try to find a way to start a fight. He was not too smart and did not know when he was walking into a losing fight. Knowing what all this would lead to, I knew that I would have to prove that certain people feared me for a reason.

Duke got up from the couch and broke me from my thoughts when he said "One more round". He seemed to be in a good mood considering everything that happened that day. When he came back, he handed me a beer and opened his. Then he flopped back down in his seat. Duke enjoyed telling us every bit of good news he had, even if it was something he wanted no one to know. That is why it did not surprise Rose or me when he jumped right back up and yelled, "I HAVE TO TELL YOU SOMETHING".

It took him a few minutes of looking at us before he would tell us what had him all excited. While Rose told people about us being engaged at the party, Jenny was naturally one of those. Jenny, who was Duke's girlfriend went to Duke and wanted to know what Duke was planning for them. That is when Duke asked her to move in with him and after she finishes her last year of school, they could move out of Ohio.

That news reminded us that we would be doing the same thing. We decided we should not let Dan and Riggs bring us down with their actions, while we planned for our future. Considering Duke was in such a great mood, we all started smiling and laughing. I called Riggs and luckily he had not left his house yet. I told him that we had too much to drink to be behind the wheel, so he should just come to my place.

Riggs agreed but did not sound happy about it. The moment I hung up, Duke grabbed the phone and called Jenny to have her come over as well. I thought I heard him ask Jenny to bring Rigg's girlfriend.

Once he finished, we went outside with a cooler full of beer and my bourbon. I opened the shed under the stairs where I kept lawn chairs and had a radio on the shelf. The radio was ideal with its dual tape player and had great sound, when it got a signal.

We sat out the chairs in the front of my place, behind my truck in the little parking lot. It did not take long and we were back to laughing and making bad jokes about Riggs and Dan. Before we knew it, the sun had set and a clear star–filled night was above us.

Rose reached into the cooler to pull out some beers, handing one to Duke and another one to me, with a kiss. While we waited for Riggs to join us, we sat watching cars going by. After fifteen minutes, Rose and Duke were talking about the wedding when I saw Riggs car pull in.

Since they did not notice Riggs pull in, I walked away and left them to talk. Riggs was sitting in his car with his hands on his face. As I stood where I could hear Duke and Rose talk while watching Riggs sitting in his car. I wondered if Riggs and Dan would want me to have the Himlee brothers put in the hospital too. Or if they wanted to take it farther. What I really feared was that once I had blood on my hands, it would not stop with the Himlee Brothers. I knew others would come, like rats. When you kill one rat, you find another one trying to come out. It takes a good plan to stop them from coming back. The first thing I would have to do was poison the pack to weaken them and wait for them to disappear.

As I thought about this, I did not notice Riggs walk up to me. When I did notice him, there he stood in front of me all beaten and a cigarette in his mouth. He put his hand on my back shoulder and without a word, we turned to walk over to Duke and Rose.

As the four of us sat under the stars, Rose sat next to me holding my hand. Riggs was nursing his bruises and a beer while sitting in the bed of my truck. Duke looked at us with a smile on his face and stood up with his beer in hand and made a toast that I will never forget. He said "Rose you are soon going to be part of this family that we have here. As part of our family that does not share blood, we are brothers held together by love and our honor. Now we have a sister who will always be a part of us, as we will always be part of you."

That led Riggs to grab another bottle of beer from the cooler and stood there for a few minutes in silence. He gave an odd look towards me and Riggs began to repeat love and honor. He repeated those words about six times. All I could think was what the hell does he know about those words.

Riggs asked me directly, what I was going to do for the honor of our family, what was I going to do to show my love. Riggs so filled with his feeling from what had happened, he also asked what I was going to do if they came after Rose.

I lost my temper and stood up out of my chair. Riggs stopped talking and sat down. He looked like a child that had done something wrong and knew he was about to be scolded.

Before I knew it, I was yelling, "Do you know what you have done? Do you know how you broke our honor and showed me no love? Do you not think that I have a reason for my actions? I would not have to worry about the Himlees as they were fading away till you and Dan decided to visit them on your own."

My face had to be as red as a tomato and I took another drink of my beer to cool down. When I started talking again, I was much calmer. I finished my lecture to Riggs by saying that I don't know how I can trust him and Dan. I warned him that, if they go behind my back again, I will treat them as I was going to treat the Himlees.

Duke and Riggs's girlfriends showed up as I finished talking. Before the girls got out of their car, I looked at Riggs and he looked as if he was not sure what to think. When his girlfriend got to him, he cheered up as she showered him with affection.

I made a comment about a "friend" from New York City that was coming into town. We were going to talk about this issue and I would finish my plan after that.

This "friend" of mine was the one who supplied me with my products and extra support if needed, as he had a large vested interest in what I did and what happened. I figured he would be bringing people to help wrap this up quickly.

We talked and drank for another three hours, then we all decided to call it a night. Riggs put his hand on my shoulder again and asked me if we could talk for a moment. We walked to Riggs car then he looked me in the eyes and told me that he was scared. He told me about how he thought that Dan and he were going to die. Riggs wrapped his arms around me and hugged me as he grasped me. He whispered in my ear that he trusts me to handle everything. When he let go, he said that he was not trying to go behind my back. Dan had made it sound to him like they were taking what I did not want, at least that's what he told me.

Riggs walked back to where Rose sat and welcomed her to our family. He gave her a hug and told her that he was sorry that this was all happening. A moment after that, Riggs got in his car with his girlfriend and drove off. Duke and his girlfriend were very drunk, so they went up to pass out on my coach. With only Rose and myself out there, I moved a chair so we would be facing each other, leaned in and kissed her.

Rose being the strong woman that she was, took my hand and said that she loved me and she is not going anywhere. Rose said "I know this is hard for you. I don't want you to worry about me. No matter what happens, I fell in love with you and want to grow old with you." I wanted to say so many different things to her, but instead I just held her hand tight.

Chapter Three

Days had passed since we had met at my place for drinks and to talk. Riggs had calmed down and Dan was just getting out of the hospital. In those few days, I had gotten quite a bit done. The most important of what needed to be done was meeting with police officers. I contributed a good amount of cash to different cops monthly. After putting things in order, I had strengthened my plan and made sure that select people were given extra attention. That left getting ready for my visitors from New York. I remember thinking that Wednesday came so quickly and after this week was over, my life would never be the same.

My guest was scheduled to come into town that night, so I made some rounds with Mick to talk with the guys on the street. We told each guy to be ready for a party at the house tonight, and how they could help us hurt the Himlee brother's business. They were happy to help once I reminded them that they would make more money afterward. After we finished, I asked Mick to get a list for me of people that work with the brothers.

For Mick, that was not a problem. We both said our goodbyes and drove off. Along the way, I stopped at a phone booth and called Duke to ask if he could meet the people coming in as I needed him to let them in. The fridge was stocked and so was the bar. Duke only asked that I bring some cookies with me. I agreed, even though I was not sure why he wanted cookies.

When I got home, I walked in my door and saw Rose sitting in my favorite chair. She was sitting there wearing an old black t–

shirt reading a book with a thin blanket over her legs. The site of her like that always made me believe that nothing was impossible. Hell, if I could get a beautiful smart girl like Rose, I could do about anything.

Rose looked up at me from her book and smiled, then sat the book down to get up to hug me. As she walked her small little cute butt over to me, I felt all the stress I was carrying melt away. It was nice to feel relaxed and what followed was also nice.

After two hours of being alone with Rose and lying in bed with each other, I was not expecting to hear people come in and make themselves at home. I got up and put a towel around my waist and grabbed a revolver, then went out to see who was in my house. When I stepped out into my living room, there was Duke, Riggs, and Dan.

With my friends sitting in my living room and Rose laying in my bed, I went from being in a great mood to wanting to kill someone. I asked Duke why he was not meeting our guest and he said that he got a call from Dan after I hung up. From what Duke said, my guest was at the house and resting.

Dan interrupted Duke with his nonsense. This was the first time I had seen Dan since the day he got himself hurt. The first thing he did when he had a chance to talk to me was blame me for what he did. I even think he was trying to get Riggs upset to the point he would turn on me.

I stood between the living room and the bedroom hallway. The sunlight from the living room windows was shining in my eyes and I needed a shower. I told them that they will get out of my house and wait for me if they wanted to talk. At that moment, I knew that they finally realized how on edge these events have made me. Anyone would have been able to pick up the anger in my tone. They got up and went outside to wait for me.

Rose came out of the bedroom with my robe on. The robe was draping off her and looked like it was four times too big for her. As Rose stood no more than 5'-4", she knew that her wearing my robe always made me laugh. This was one of the many reasons that I wanted to spend the rest of my life with her. All I could think of as she handed me my clothes, was that I have to protect those that I call my family.

After a quick shower, I kissed her goodbye and walked out the door to where Riggs, Duke, and Dan was sitting. As I walked down the wooden steps, they all were sitting on the tailgate of my pickup, smoking. I hated this because they always threw the cigarette butts in my truck bed, making it look like a large ashtray.

They sat there smoking and joking around with each other. Duke looked up as I walked towards them and I threw my keys to Duke. Dan looked up at me with a serious look on his face. When I finally stepped off the last step, Dan stood up, pulled his keys out of his pocket and walked to his car without saying a word to me. Riggs and Duke stood up as Duke got into the driver's seat of my truck. Riggs came and spoke to me for a moment. After our conversation, Riggs walked over to Dan's car and I walked to the passenger side of my truck.

As I was getting into my truck, I knew that my plans that would lead me to either being dead or killing someone. At that point, I considered both could happen. I guess anything could have happened, and I honestly dreaded the meeting.

Duke drove down the road and I sat lost in my thoughts. Before I realized it, Duke pulled into the house and gave me a little shove to bring me back into the real world.

I remember telling Duke that this meeting was going to be the first step into something bad. It will be something I would never be able to turn back from. As I hung my head down a bit, Duke put his hand on my back and told me to remember to be strong for everyone. Duke finished his pep talk with saying "as you're being strong holding everyone up, I will be strong holding you up." Duke smacked me on the chest and got out of the truck.

Perhaps you are wondering why I do not live in this house. I bought this property for fifteen thousand off a police auction. It wasn't in the best of shape, but it worked for meetings and provided my guys a place to stay if they needed it. This house was where my out of town guest was staying too. The house was not meant to be a permanent place to live. I also listed it under my legal business. I learned from Deatz who was the guy I took over for, that if you don't show where you make money, people will start looking more into you.

There was an hour before Riggs and Dan would show and then another hour before Mick and his guys would be showing up. That meant I should have enough time to get everything taken care of. I walked into the house and asked Duke to join me. Once inside, the main guy from New York introduced everyone and told Duke that he could call him John.

After forty-five minutes of talking with the guys, one of the property alarms went off. Without a word, Duke went to see who it was and let us finish talking. I am glad that none of John's guys went to check because they all seemed to have a gun on them and they weren't well hidden.

Duke came back into the back room and John got up to leave. I told John that I would talk in private with Duke before I could join him. I sat quietly waiting for everyone to leave the room. Then I told Duke "I don't trust anyone else to know this. What we discussed could possibly happen and I need you to help me if it does. You cannot tell anyone what you know, not now or ever. This will be something to take to the grave."

I let Duke sit in the room by himself to think about everything. I wish I could have given him more time, but I needed to get Riggs and Dan. I needed to make sure they would not do anything to get in our way or screw up things. As long as they listened to me, I could hopefully get everything straightened out. Before I walked out of the room, I looked back and noticed Duke seemed to be a bit sick.

I walked into the living room and saw Dan talking to John as he was saying how important he was with my business. I could tell that he did not know who John was, but was trying to look important. He knew that people that came to these parties were open to talking. All I could think was how Dan never knew when to shut his mouth.

Riggs on the other hand knew to watch what was going on

around him and listened to what was being said before speaking. That is why Riggs noticed me standing on the opposite side of the living room. He got up and got Dan's attention. Once they both were looking at me, I opened the door to the room Duke was in and I waited for them to come in.

We walked in the room and when Dan saw Duke sitting in the room already, he started to bitch more. I did everything to hold my temper till I shut the door after Riggs and Dan got into the room. That is when I grabbed Dan and pushed him up against the wall. Without thinking, I pulled my knife and had it to the side of his head. My hands were full of his shirt and my knuckles were pushing into Dan's chest. I told him that he is not calling the shots and that he better remember that. I reminded him that he can't do what needed done; no matter how tough he thought he was. I also reminded him that I fully trusted Duke, where I had little trust in him after what he pulled. With fire in my eyes, I told him to sit down and shut up. I let go of him and everyone sat down at the table, including Dan.

They all were surprised to see a hidden shelf was behind a cheap picture of a ship in rough waters that I had hung up. The shelf had a personal stash of Jameson eighteen year old whiskey and weed. I pulled both out and handed them to Duke. Duke poured shots for everyone and Dan started to roll two joints. One of the joints was for him and Duke to share, and the other was for just me. I'm sure Dan realized that I was in the worst mood he had ever seen me in.

When I sat down at the table, there was a shot and a joint in front of me. I lit up the joint and Riggs asked me if I could wait to smoke it. I just looked at Riggs and took a hit of the joint. I knew Riggs liked to say he never did drugs, but always enjoyed the contact high he got. Everyone enjoyed the time and relaxed. I began to tell Dan and Riggs how they were going to help me by staying out of my business. Their job in this plan was to find out when the brothers were apart from each other. After giving them the details of what they needed to do, I asked everyone to leave me alone for a bit. They all agreed and left quietly.

I poured myself another shot and put everything away. Sitting back down in my chair, my head fell into my right hand. My left hand holding my glass of whiskey and an unlit cigarette down to my side. I don't know how long I sat there, but John walked into the room and looked at me. As I lifted my head out of my hand, he shut the door behind himself and sat down next to me. He told me that he knows that this will be hard, but it will be the only way to protect those that are involved. John reminded me that he would be there after I am done to put things in order. He got up, grabbed my arm and lifted me up.

I took my shot and walked out to a room full of people as I followed John. As I walked into a crowded room that was loud with chatter and laughter, people noticed I was there, and the room got quiet. While all my guys looked at me, Mick walked over to stand by my side. Before I said anything, Mick started the meeting as was customary with all our meetings.

Mick said to everyone "We don't tell anyone what we do here. What happens is only for us to know so we can make more money. Bearman can explain what is going on. So listen up." I reached out and put my hand on Mick's shoulder as he sat back down in his chair. I think Mick was trying to act like a hard ass, but everyone knew he would help any of them if they needed it.

As I stood up in front of twenty–some guys, I looked around the room. I saw that they were all waiting to hear what was going to be done over the conflict the brothers started. I turned and looked at Riggs and Dan, then I began to speak to the whole room.

"We are not here to pour gas on a fire. Pouring gas on the fire and expecting that to stop the fire does not work. With that kind of thinking, we may as well also pour gas on everything we built. I love a good bon fire, but I don't want to use my home for the kindling."

After a moment of thought, I continued to speak. "There are many kinds of fires and the trick is knowing how to put the fire out as quickly as you can. You don't want to let a fire spread. A fire needs two things to keep going: Oxygen and fuel. We will make it hard for this fire to find air to breathe and remove anything it needs as fuel. When we are finished, no one will be crazy enough to even light a match without checking with us from now on. The fear of God will not compare to the fear people will have for us."

John stood up and introduced one of the guys that came with him. John said that his guy will be staying behind to watch his interest in Ohio. The guy looked dark and hateful; he was introduced as Ferris. Ferris stood just a bit above six foot; a scarred chin, slightly above average build, and long dark brown hair. When John finished, Ferris spoke to my guys. "I am here to help grow the area and support Bearman however I can. Together we will make more money. I will also let people know that you guys have the support of all of us in New York." He did not build any trust with the guys, but you could see that he felt he did a good job.

While Ferris was talking, I told Mick that he needs to let the guys know that Ferris was just below him. I let Mick know that Duke will be stepping in for me collecting money. Then I let Mick know that I will have Ferris help me with organizing the product. After going through what changes were taking place, Mick only had one thing to say. He said, "I will do what you need me to, as long as you keep making me money."

By the time Mick and I finished talking, Ferris finished his speech. Mick stood up and said, "A keg is tapped in the back of Bearman's truck bed. The toolbox has party favors in a brown box. Why are you all still in here?"

It took nothing more for the guys to rush outside like a group of school kids. Some stopped to talk with Mick, but none of them hung around for long.

Mick came up to me while I was talking with Duke, Dan, Riggs, and Ferris. Mick reached his hand out to Ferris and told him that hopefully they can work well together. Mick was a good guy to have to work for me.

Mick and Ferris talked for a bit and went outside to join everyone else. It was not long before Duke, Dan, and Riggs went out as well. With everyone outside enjoying the party, I went to my truck to grab my flask. When I got to my truck, there was John with the remaining guys he had brought with him loading up their cars. They had come in a car that sat in the garage while they were there. I decided to have one last talk with John before he left.

John told me that they would be going back to New York that night. There was some business they had to deal with. I guess they had complete trust in Ferris, so they did not care to stay around. I said my goodbyes and went on my way to join everyone else at the party.

Before I got to where everyone was, one of the guys who worked under Mick ran up to me screaming. When I calmed him down, he said that Mick had been stabbed. I followed this guy to where Mick laid on the ground bleeding. I started yelling at the guys who were standing in shock. I took off my flannel shirt and pressed it against his stomach where he was stabbed. Soon one of the guys drove up in a car. We loaded Mick into the car as I told Mick that I would take care of everything and all he needed to do was to hang on. Mick grabbed my arm and pulled me close to tell me that he wants to be the one who kills the bitch who knifed him.

I promised him that he can do whatever he wanted, to whoever did this. Ferris got in the car. He and another guy were taking Mick to the hospital. As Ferris was about to shut his door, I told him that he needs to go with his new cousin for this farming accident. He needs to explain that he fell on something on the farm and you don't know what it is called. Ferris nodded, then they drove off.

Once they were out of sight, I turned to everyone and demanded that someone better bring me whoever stabbed Mick. Within a minute, some of the guys dragged this girl in front of me. Her hands were covered in blood and dressed like one of the prostitutes or common girls I invited. It was clear that she had been working for drugs and she was high on something. She had been on something for a few years and yet could not be much older than 20.

To be honest, I was shocked that it was a girl high off her ass that had stabbed Mick. I stood there beyond angry and thinking about Riggs & Dan being beaten up. Now Mick being stabbed, I was more afraid of my rage than anything else. I had never dealt with this level of rage before. I grabbed Duke and told him to lock her in the basement; just make sure no one touches her till Mick gets to her.

As Duke had two guys grab the girl and drag her away, he stopped them and asked her why she stabbed Mick. I walked closer to hear what she said. Lighting up my cigarette, I heard her start to cry. She started telling how Jay Himlee promised her that she would never have to pay for drugs again if she stabbed me. She said she did not know what I looked like, so she mistook Mick for me. Mick had a lot of people around him. I think she figured whoever had the most people around them was the boss.

Jay Himlee was the younger brother that attacked Riggs and Dan. I always considered Jay to be too scared to do anything himself, yet he also was unpredictable. Now if this brown haired skinny piece of shit wanted to bring a full war, he was going to get what he wanted.

Finally, I started to walk to my truck and when I opened my door, I looked at my crowbar. I let my anger take control of me and grabbed it. I walked back to the group of my guys yelling and foaming at the mouth to get revenge. Everyone parted when they saw me coming and everyone got quiet when I stood in front of her.

Duke looked at me and said, "The brothers were coming after us. Mick was the first one she got to tonight." Then Duke stepped out of my way. I took the final step to her and squatted down to her. Putting my hand under her chin and lifting up her head, I whispered in her ear, "I promise you that you will never have to pay for drugs too. No one will rape you or do anything without my permission, but you will not enjoy being here." Then I wrapped the hook of the crowbar around her armpit and dragged her to the back door of the house. She laid on the ground now covered in mud, tears, and fear. I unhooked her and told one of the guys to take her down to the basement and out of my sight.

Duke, Dan, and Riggs walked up behind me and told everyone that she was only to be given a little bit of food. Duke was the one that everyone would listen to out of the three of them, and he made sure everyone knew not to touch her. Dan stopped four guys and told them that they would watch the girl for now. Dan gave them instructions and he left with Riggs to go home. Everyone left as well and it was only Duke and me.

Duke grabbed the crowbar from my hand and directed me back to my truck. We got into my truck and again, I had Duke drive because of what happened. I could not focus enough to drive. On the drive back to my place, I said that I wanted to have Riggs or Dan go see Mick in the hospital. Have them tell Mick that we got the girl and also tell Mick that he can do whatever he wants to her; just not kill her. I have a plan and I am going to need the girl in the end. With a smile on my face, I sat back in the passenger seat.

Chapter Four

I think back now to the moment that I knew what I would do to Jay Himlee. The fact that I wanted to make him suffer, and I had planned to do it in the worse way I could. I was a bit frightened of how happy I was with myself with the plan and how well I slept that night.

I woke up and called to get any news on Mick I could. Mick was OK and fixed up. He spent the night in the hospital and was released. Knowing that, I got around to go check on the girl to make sure she was not raped or dead. When I arrived, John was already gone and Ferris sat in my living room. As he sat on the couch drinking some coffee, he had a smile on his face. I sat next to him and told one of the guys that stayed at the house to get me my coffee. Ferris said he was going to enjoy being in Ohio.

Before I could ask why, a girl walked out of the bedroom and he gave me a shoulder nudge. I waited a moment for her to walk out of the house, and then I told him to go get checked. When I referred to a girl as a common girl, those are girls invited to parties. These girls normally show up to see if they could get some free drugs or do stuff for some cash to get drugs. I would occasionally set up dates for the girls. Those girls tended to have some sort sexual disease and most of the guys ended up at the doctor's office.

Ferris tried to explain that he doesn't believe that country girls are that way. Without saying anything, I got up and went to go down to check on the girl who stabbed Mick. As I grabbed the door handle to go into the basement, Ferris told me that Mick was already downstairs. This did not settle easily in my gut. I feared that Mick would kill the girl and mess up my plan. However, if Mick did kill her, I could not be upset.

When I opened the basement door, there sat Mick on the bottom step and I was kind of shocked to see him sitting there and staring at the girl. It looked creepy as hell to see him like that, but I knew he had to be thinking of hurting and killing that girl. Even against my urge not to go down to the basement, I still walked down the stairs and sat next to him.

After about 10 minutes of Mick making grunt noises and crunching his face, I finally told him that I had a plan. He asked if I needed her for it. I replied by saying I could work around things if she was not around. I told him my plan for the girl and promised Mick that he will get to finish the job if he can wait. I could tell that Mick was happy with what was going to happen. He smiled a bit and went back upstairs.

With everything in order, I was not in the mood to stay at the house, so I went to Findlay to meet up with Duke. He had some money for me and said that some police chief in the area wanted to talk to me. I got in my truck and started to drive. Some of Himlee's guys must have been waiting for me. After a few miles down the road, a car sped past me and another started to ride my bumper. Then the car that sped past was turned sideways and blocked the road. I knew that Himlee's guys usually only carried knives and bats.

I slowed down my truck to a crawl and waited till the car behind me stopped. I was about to face a group of guys that I could only imagine had been told to attack me any chance they could. This confirmed that the brothers wanted to take me out. I figured the Himlee brothers thought they could take over my business by killing me or scare me out of the area.

Thinking about this, I stopped my truck between the two cars and watched two guys get out of the car behind me, then four from the car blocking the road in front of me. These bastards thought they were a group of tough guys. That was, until I got out of my truck. I had to show these guys that if they wanted to come after me and mine; I would make sure that everyone involved would pay. I heard one of the guys in front of my truck yell that they were going to mess me over worse than what my friend got. This pissed me off more than I already was. Without a word in reply to them, I pulled out my gun and shot one guy in the leg and another one in the arm. When I turned to the guys behind me, I saw them getting in their cars driving away and I put another two bullets into the back of their car. As quickly as they came, both cars were gone.

Now with seeing that the brother's guys coming after me, I made a side trip to my mom's and stepdad's house. I wanted to pick up some guns that I had hidden away in an old barn that my great grandpa built when he was farming. I did not expect to see anyone at my parents' house, but my step-dad Paul was home. As I pulled in, Paul was watching me drive down the driveway from the side of the barn.

I did not want to run into anyone, but both my mom and Paul were always there for me and I enjoyed talking with them. When I got out of my truck, Paul yelled over to me to have me give him a hand with lifting a big piece of a tree that they had cut down. After we loaded some of the wood on his trailer, we sat on the railing of the trailer and talked for about an hour.

I began to get up and started to walk to the barn when Paul stopped me and asked what I was doing. I said I had an old box out at the barn and was going to meet up with Duke. He said that I should remember to clean the guns or I might have problems. Being shocked that he knew what I was hiding, I asked him how he knew. He asked what it was and I said it was a box of playboys a buddy asked if he could have. Paul turned away and walked into the house to clean up and make a sandwich for lunch.

Without another word, I got the box and put them in the back seat of my truck. As I was about to get into my truck to leave, Paul came back out and handed me a bottle of homemade wine and a sandwich. He told me to enjoy the wine with Rose and give her his love, and he also told me that he was happy she was going to be part of our family. Paul and my mom both loved Rose as much as I did. I smiled, sat the bottle on my seat, and gave him a big hug. I did not want to let him go, but I did and got into my truck to drive away.

As I drove down route twenty-three going through Fostoria, I saw a guy who got his product from us and sold it on his own. He was walking down county line road when I saw him. He had been late turning in his money for the product that Mick gave him. I stopped and called him over to me; when he got over to my truck, I told him to get in to take a ride with me. He got in the truck like I told him and I drove on to Findlay. While we went down the road, I asked if he had any friends in Findlay and he told me that he had a few friends there. I smiled and reminded him that he owed Mick fifteen hundred dollars, which means he owes me money.

We drove a bit more, and then he told me that he would get the money. He had a scared look on his face, but considering that my gun was sitting in the cup holder, I could not blame him. When I noticed him looking at the gun, I put it away in the center console. I told him that he can work off the money if he does manual labor work for me. In fact, he also needs another person who doesn't know me or anyone that works for me. He agreed, but it was because he knew the penalty for not paying was much worse then somebody would like to deal with. In fact, the last guy who owed me money was found naked on the side of the road screaming from a bad acid trip and a broken arm. He should not have watched the movie Ring while tripping.

For the rest of the drive, we did not speak. I sang some 80's songs that were on the radio. The poor guy had to deal with my singing, but we finally arrived where Duke was waiting. Before the guy got out of my truck, I had him write down his contact info. I told him that I wanted the money if I don't call him in two weeks. From our discussion and him knowing the penalty for owing me money, he would wait for me to reach out to him. Sadly, I did not know his name was James until that moment. James walked away quickly and Duke got in my truck with a backpack that he put in my back seat next to the box.

Duke asked me what that guy was doing with me and I told him "He is going to dig a few holes for me." Duke shook his head and we talked for a bit about other things. I told Duke about the brothers putting another hit on me and maybe on everyone else. I reached into the box and pulled out a 9mm, then handed it to him.

When I told him about my day, he told me that the gun will not leave his side. I thanked him for everything and asked him if he could meet at the bridge that evening. He said he was free and asked if he should bring Dan and Riggs with him. I nodded yes and Duke got out of my truck. I don't know where he went from there.

Since I was done talking to Duke, I wanted to get going so I could get to my place. I stopped at a deli in Fostoria for a quick sandwich along my way to Fremont where I had to meet someone. While I waited for my food, the police chef of Fostoria came in to get something as well. The food was what he came in for, but he was happy to see me sitting there. He walked over to my table and sat down. He started to laugh and talked about what was going on in Fostoria. We joked and talked for an half hour as we eat; when we finished our food, I asked him to wait while I went to get something from my truck. Within a few minutes, I came back in and I gave him a book. I knew he would like the book because between each page had a twenty dollar bill for bookmarks. I put a twenty on the table and got up. When I started to walk away, I said that the brothers were making it hard to buy bigger books for his library. I was out the deli's doors, as I wanted to get stuff done and get home.

When I got to my truck, there was a cop sitting on the tailgate smoking a cigarette. I did not notice that the cop was a guy I knew from school who was two years ahead of me until I sat down next to him. He smiled at me and asked if I knew anything about two guys being shot out in the country. I lit up a cigarette and told him that I knew a bit about it. All I could say to him was, "From what I know, some of the Himlee brother's guys were after someone and trapped him. You know if you're trapped by a bunch of guys that want to do some serious damage, you would probably fire a few shots too."

I had nothing more to say and asked him if we needed to talk more about this. Since he got his pot from me, he told me to have a good day and put the lid back on the box in my back seat. We stood up and put up the tailgate and I got in my truck. The cop walked by my door and gave me his cell phone number and told me if I need help, he is not always a cop. All I could do was smile and thank him. It got a bit creepy as he kept standing there, so I put my truck in gear and told him to let me know if he ever needs anything.

As I drove down the road, I started to think about how the movies made being the head of a crime organization look romantic and exciting. I guess what you don't see in the movies are the little things needing to be done and all the people have to be dealt with. By the time I finished my thoughts, I reached a coffee house on the edge of Fremont. I was going to meet up with someone before finally going home. I walked in and saw Mark Himlee sitting at a table.

Now Mark Himlee is the brother who had the brains and was level headed but did not have a stomach for violence. Mark has been in some fights and there was a fight when we had each other's back. He never liked violence and blood. From what I was told, he is the one who stopped Riggs and Dan from ending up worse than they were. I honestly liked Mark and hung out with him a few times when we would run drugs for another guy. The guy we both were running for ended up dying in a car accident and the car fire. That is what was being said, but he was trying to play to different mobs at the same time.

I met John about that same time. The Same time Mark met some guys from Chicago. Since then Mark and I ended up working with these people and became competitors. For a while, we would try to work together so we did not step on each other's toes. That changed when we both started gaining ground and making more money. Soon we started to go to the towns that we had agreed to let the others have.

Now back to the cafe. As I was standing outside, I wondered how it will go with Mark and me in the same place. I looked up and saw him waving me to come in to join him. Since I was going to meet the Police chief of Fremont.   I had to go in. So I joined Mark and ordered myself a large mocha.

I sat down my coffee and another book full of my favorite bookmarks. Mark said, "We need to talk about where we are heading. " I just started to laugh and asked if he means having people come after me and those close to me. He had nothing to say about that. With the silence bothering me, I said that he and his brother started us going down this road. I found it interesting that Mark said that he did not want this, but he knew that his brother started this. His problem was, Mark would not give up his brother freely so we can resolve this issue. If he did, this story would have been much different.

We discussed what all has happened and what will most likely happen. Then we spoke of rules that will have to be upheld by both sides. We kept our rules that we referred to as the rules of conduct to a few key rules. The main thing was that the family that is not involved in our business was off limits. This includes friends and girlfriends. The other rule that I found important was that no one was to use a gun for any reason in a town. We did not want innocent people getting hurt.

After we finished talking, Mark got up to leave and said: "tell the police chief I said hello." I simply replied with "tell Jay he should expect visitors." Mark did not like that. Jay was more of Mark's business as any other person. Plus I owed Jay for the attempts that he recently made. Mark knew this and knew Jay got himself into this.

With Mark gone and the police chief of Fremont running late, I ordered two mochas to go. Then asked to delay the order for fifteen minutes or so while I finished the one I was having. That is when the police chief walked in. The waitress stopped walking away and turned to ask if my guest would like anything. Before she said anything, he raised his hand to signal he wanted nothing.

This police chief was one of my customers. He not only liked my drugs, but he also enjoyed one of the girls that worked as a "common girl" for me. In fact, I knew he was in a bit of a hurry to meet with a certain girl, so he sat down and got straight to business. He asked if the book was for him when I nodded yes to his question, he slid the book over to himself. He ordered a drink to go and we talked till both of our drinks came. We both walked out to our vehicles when I stopped him and told him that the brothers don't know the things that I do.

If I find out that he is accepting money from anyone other than me, I will not be able to keep all his secrets. He told me to go to Hell. Then said if I wanted, he would push more enforcement on the people that are known to work for the Himlee brothers. I smiled and said that it would be nice to see the streets of Fremont being cleaned up a bit.

Without another word, we drove off in different directions. The nice thing is I did not live far from Fremont. I lived between two small farm towns, Risingsun which is where I grew up and Gibsonburg. I personally try to stay out of Gibsonburg, since that is where the people who shared my last name live. Those people were the type of people you would picture when you think of rednecks. Don't get me wrong, even though they were rednecks, there was one or two that was fun to be around. I could not tell you if they could be trusted, but I did not put any trust in any of them to be safe.

I am getting off topic, but when thinking of Gibsonburg, there are not too many good memories from that town. After a quick 20 minute drive, I was back at my place and Rose was sitting outside reading a book. I gave her a kiss and handed her the mocha I had gotten for her. I started to walk up the stairs and looked back to see Rose before I went into the apartment. I did love seeing her smile when she looked at the cup. She saw a note I wrote for her that just said, "Till my dying breath". Knowing she liked what I wrote, I went into the apartment and reloaded my gun.

Closing the door behind me, I started thinking as I stood in a half-lighted room with the sun shining through the half-open blinds. I stood there holding my gun and feeling like I was on the edge of getting sick till Rose came in and yelled at me. She came over to me and swung herself around me pulling us very close together. She kissed my neck and said that we have to go to the bridge.

I held the gun out of sight and put it into my back holster clipped to the back of my jeans. Looking back, when I was young and in love, it is amazing how much I could not get enough of being close to people. But, that is not important now. I guess what is important is the knock on my screen door and hearing it open and slamming shut. Hearing someone coming in when I did not expect anyone did not help me from being on edge.

My luck! It was a pissed off Mick. I kissed Rose on the head and asked if she would grab a beer for all of us, then Mick and I sat down to talk. The first thing Mick said was "You made an agreement with Mark Himlee? It's his brother that got me stabbed and from what I hear, their guys came after you today." Rose walked in with the beers and heard that I had some guys come after me. He kept talking about how I only got away unharmed because I had a gun on hand.

Mick shut up when he realized that Rose was upset. He had informed her about a part of my day that I was not going to tell her about. She did not need to know these things. Rose put the beers on the coffee table and sat down next to me. Mick feeling bad, now asked Rose to let us talk in private. Rose chuckled and said that she knows about what I do now and she is not going anywhere.

Before letting them get into a debate of her staying, I told Mick that I ran into Mark Himlee in Fremont that day. That agreement he and I made was to protect the people around us that are not involved in the shit we do. "We are in a war now with the Himlee brothers. We agreed that only the people who work pushing drugs, hooking, and running our game rooms need to worry about themselves. If some outsider gets hurt, Mark or I will need to handle the person that did it. What Mark and I agreed on, is if this is not done is something neither of us wants." After Mick heard this from me, he asked what will happen next.

I pulled a piece of paper out of my pocket without a word. It had all the things Mark Himlee and I agreed upon written in ink. We both signed each other's copies to show we were in agreement. I handed Mick the paper and told him that he was going to go visit the guest at the house. I asked Mick to get copies made of the agreement to give to our guys. I wanted everyone, including our house guest, to have a copy.

Tired of all the crap that happened during the day, I finished my beer, got up and went into my bedroom to change my clothes. A summer night can still get a chill, so it was smart to have a long sleeve shirt; that also helps keep the bugs from biting. I had to get ready to meet Duke, Dan, and Riggs. I came back out and Mick was gone; Rose was standing by the door grabbing our flannels from the hangers for us to leave. I asked how she knew about my meeting with the guys. She was pissed about what Mick had said, but she told me that Duke called. He told her about our meeting and wanted me to know that all the girlfriends were going to be there. I did not know the girls were coming. I was glad she told me.

Having the girlfriends coming with us to meet under the bridge was not something I wanted. I did not want to give Dan and Riggs the guns I had for them with their girls around, but I have no choice. It seemed that I was trapped in my own mind a lot since Dan and Riggs got put in the hospital. Without realizing it Rose was driving us down the road for a night to spend with friends. Rose must have figured her driving would get my mind off the Himlee brothers. She must have believed I needed to clear my head before we met with our friends. Rose did not realize that the back seat had two handguns loaded and ready for Dan & Riggs.

Within a short time, we got to the bridge and I heard everyone laughing, talking, and playing music. It was great to hear everyone having a good time. I decided that I was going to have a good time myself, at least for Rose's benefit.

To be honest, a bit into getting there, I was having a great time.

It was like nothing changed and there was nothing to worry about. It was a great night until I stepped away for a moment. I walked up the gravel covered hill to stand on the street and clear my head. When I got up there, I saw Jay Himlee with a few guys leaning against a car.

When Jay saw me, he yelled at me and started to storm over to me. His guys stayed behind, but I noticed them pull out guns and set them on the car. I must have been lucky because Duke and his girlfriend was off for some private time. Duke saw Jay heading my way and had his girlfriend go grab Riggs and Dan so I had some help. Duke remembered that I had guns in my truck. As everyone ran in my direction, Duke got into my truck and gave Dan and Riggs a gun each. Then they continued to me.

When they got up to me, Jay was standing in front of me. Jay was pissed like Mick was. I could only assume that his brother told him of our agreement. Jay was screaming at me about me talking to his brother. As I listened to him rant, the asshole pulled out his gun and pointed it towards my chest. I stepped closer to him and he pushes the gun more into my chest. As I looked over Jay's shoulder, I saw that his guys had their guns in their hands. Jay continued telling me what he thought and how I should have my guys put their guns down.

It did not help that I was drunk and high. I learned that staying calm can help get through most problems. Not being in the mood to deal with any more of Jay's stupid stunts, I decided to make sure he knew how big of a mistake he made. So with a big smile on my face, I pulled out a cigarette from my pocket and lit it and blew smoke in Jay's face. I told him that he is playing with a friend of the devil and I am not afraid of going to see my friend.

Jay got a scared look on his face and stepped back. His guys were yelling and so were my buddies, but Jay looked into my eyes and started to turn white. I slid my gun from my back and shoved it in his nuts. With the smile on my face, I told him that he might kill me, but I will make sure that he can never have sex again. I began to laugh at him and told him that living with nothing below the waist would not be much different from now.

That moment I knew I had Jay Himlee where I wanted him. He turned and walked away. I yelled over to Jay and told him that next time the smart brother makes a deal without him, he should be a man. He should go talk to the person he has a problem with.

As those guys drove away, Duke and Riggs came up while Dan went back to the girls. Duke asked if I was OK. The only thing I said as I looked at Riggs was he needs to see Mick tomorrow. Since Riggs did not know what was going on, Riggs gave me a blank look and asked, why?

The best answer I had to say was "Tell Mick that he can have fun on Saturday the 15th. Without another word, we went back to our girlfriends and called it a night. It was in fact 1:00 in the morning, so we all went home or to someone's home.

Chapter Five

The sun came up and started shining through my window. The warmth on my face woke me up to see Rose sitting in the corner of the room in an old rocking chair.

As I sat up in bed and wiping the sleep from my eyes, I asked Rose what was wrong. Before she had time to answer, the thought of an angry fiancée was not how I wanted to start my day.

Rose told me that she knew the following day was when I started to go after the Himlee brothers and put an end to the fighting that had begun. She said that a dream woke her . It was a bad dream a few hours ago. Within seconds of saying that, she jumped from the chair and on top of me. Rose was in tears by the time she tackled me back to my pillow.

I asked her again what was wrong. Then she told me that she was afraid that this whole thing was going to kill me and she dreamed she was standing at my grave.

With her head shoved into my neck and crying, I held her tight till she fell asleep. I could only assume that she was worn out from not getting much sleep and the stress she felt from her dream. As she slept, I got up to make some breakfast. I don't know why I remember making scrambled eggs with garlic grilled onions and some sausages so well, but I do.

While I was putting the food on the plate, I heard a knock on the door. I was not expecting anyone; I got a bit worried who was at the door. Walking over to the door, I picked up my gun.

Looking through the window, I saw Duke and Mick standing outside waiting to be let in.

Opening the door for them to come in, Duke started to talk to me about what was going on about the Himlees. Both Duke and Mick sat on the couch, then I had them quiet their voices down since Rose was sleeping. Not wanting Rose to wake up, once they lowered their voices, I told them that Rose was sleeping. They said OK and did not get too loud again.

Duke handed me a folded up piece of paper. When I grabbed it, he said that some of the Himlee brother's guys wanted to work for us. On the paper was the names of those guys. With the yellow piece of paper, I went into the kitchen to start cooking and making coffee.

I opened the paper, looked, closed it, and then I asked why I should care about these names. "We are a day away from starting to put the Himlee's out of business and removing all the people in our way. These people will either be in jail, hiding from us, or come to use to work for us to get their supplies. Again, why do I care about these people?"

Mick stood up and took the paper from the counter where I laid it. He opened it and pointed to the fourth name on the list. Sure as shit, I had a reason to care once I realized whose name Mick was pointing towards. That name was one of Jay Himlee's closest friends. So, I told them that I want to talk to him today.

Duke started to smile and said, "I figured you would, so I told Riggs to bring him to the deli in Fostoria. Before we left to come here, Riggs called and said that they will be there for lunch."

I asked Mick and Duke if he might be able to let us know where Jay Himlee would be. Rose walked into the room wearing one of my shirts and a pair of her cotton short shorts. I told Duke and Mick that I will see them for lunch. They understood that they should leave and let me enjoy my breakfast with Rose.

As they left and I closed the door behind them, I turned around to see Rose eating my food. Just to mess with her, I walked over and grabbed the plate and asked why is she eating my food. She stabbed my arm a little bit and smiled at me.

Since I was fully aware that I lost my breakfast, I went back into the kitchen and started to cook myself some more eggs. Rose came in and asked me if my lunch meeting she heard I had planned would be a good thing or bad. Putting my eggs on the plate again, I told her that it could be a very good thing. I joked that we could run away to a far off place and live on a beach or in the mountains.

We spent the rest of that morning cuddled up together on the recliner and talking. It was a good morning for me and I was hoping that the rest of my day would follow in the same manner. Then as I had to get around, I got in the shower and shaved to look nicer than the rough look I normally have. When I meet my possible new friend, I want him to feel relaxed around me.

Feeling better after my shower, I walked out of the bathroom wearing my favorite blue towel and saw Ferris sitting talking to Rose. This was the first time that Rose had meet Ferris and she was interested in his stories of New York City. When I cleared my throat, he looked up at me from my recliner and said he was coming to have lunch with me.

Shocked that he knew what was going on, I asked how he knew what I planned for my lunch. He told me about how Dan had come to the house to check on Ferris. Ferris said he was checking to see if he wanted anything. Since I did not want anything said in front of Rose, I did not ask any other questions at that time and went to finished getting dressed. From what I could hear, Rose and Ferris went back to talk about New York City and how the city had a life of its own. Personally, I felt New York was too crowded and dirty.

While they talked, I did something that was out of my norms and sat on the edge of the bed. I began to pray; saying "I don't know if anyone is listening to me or if this will do any good. If someone is listening, I don't want my family to pay for my sins. I don't expect to be forgiven for the things I have done. I just want my family to be safe and out of harm's way."

I chuckled thinking about how I would have made fun of someone who did what I did.

Once I was dressed I took a deep breath, stood up, and walked out to the living room. As Ferris was telling Rose about ice skating during Christmas time at Rockefeller center. I gave him a push on his back. He stood up and walked out of the door. I gave Rose a kiss and as I was about to walk out, Rose told me that she wanted to ice skate that winter. I could only smile and said that it would be nice.

By the time I got out of the house Ferris was sitting in my truck waiting for me. I really did not want to deal with him. I also was thinking I need to start locking my truck. I guess since John sent Ferris here to be his eyes and ears and he worked for John instead of me, I should play nice.

After a short drive and some pointless conversation with Ferris, we got to the deli. Ferris was about to get out of my truck, I asked him why Dan had come to tell him about what I was doing. He asked why I need to know; as long as he knows what is happening is all that matters.

Being on edge to start with, I grabbed his shoulder and told him that it matters. I finished with telling him "if I don't know who I can't trust, then I will not trust anyone and even your small mind can see how that will be a problem." With that said, Ferris pulled himself away from me and said Dan made a deal with him so he will not be left out in the cold. He got out of my truck and walked towards the deli.

I was seeing red at the fact that a friend of mine would betray me again. I have let Dan into my close circle through Riggs. Dan went to join Ferris when he thought it would benefit him. I guess I was not too surprised that Dan would of did this. Even though my heart felt very heavy and my anger built up in me, I had to put it all aside. At that point, I had to focus on getting information that could help me.

As I open the door to the deli; I saw Ferris sitting next to Dan, Riggs, and Duke. They were sitting on the other side of the table next to Jay Himlee's right-hand man and best friend. They all were looking at me afraid of what I might do. From their looks, I think that they figured I was about to kill someone. This was not far from the truth with Dan sitting there trying to get one over on me and the reason for all this shit. I understand that Jay Himlee would have found something else to start our fight. I also know that Mark would have not backed his brother for something stupid though.

I walked past the table and ordered some food before joining everyone. It was a slow day for the deli and the only other customer was paying her bill. When I sat down, I heard the lady began to walk out with her heels clicking on the tile flooring.

I used to like that deli; I would be able to have some quiet talks with people about the subject I wanted to keep personal. It did not hurt that I liked the coffee and meatloaf they made. The owner might have had an idea about what I did. He came to me one day telling me that he doesn't care what people say I do for my money. He did not want me to bring any troubles into the deli. I promised him that any trouble that might happen would not be from me. I later let Mick tell people to not sell at this deli or start anything.

The reason that I liked that deli is not really important, I simply like to remember it. What is important is what was said shortly after I received my coffee. Jay Himlee's best friend, let's call him Timmy, spoke up and asked why so many people had to be there. Dan went to say something, but Ferris spoke up and said that he is new to the area. He also said that he asked these other guys to meet him so they could go somewhere after.

This seemed to calm down Timmy. Timmy started to talk about why he was jumping ship and getting away from Jay. I did not ask a question, but Timmy told me everything. Stories of how out of control Jay was getting with his drinking and mixing different drugs.

I had a feeling that Timmy was trying to play both sides so he could come out OK or avoid getting hurt. I was not sure what he would tell Jay or Mark after he leaves the deli. I explained to Timmy who Ferris was. I expect that he had gone over it many times and knew it as it really happened.

All I could do was smile at him and say, "Thank you. I know

you would like to know what I have planned for you. What I need you to do is be able to tell a story and keep to it. If you don't, then you will go from not being a thought to me, and instead you will go to the top of my personal list." Timmy looked confused and asked what story he would need to remember. I just told him that I or someone will tell him what to say and who to tell it to. I told Timmy that I wanted him to play both sides. It's a win–win for him and I am guessing that is what he wanted.

While everyone at the table was confused about why I was giving Timmy a way to play both sides, I left the table. I went to the counter for one last cup of coffee and the food I ordered to go. I was going back to spending the rest of my day with Rose once I finished talking to Timmy. That is when Dan came up to me to ask what I was thinking. Since I was far from happy with Dan at that point, I instructed him to go ask the guy he is working for now.

"What the hell do you mean by that?" Dan yelled and continued on with, "I have always been with you and you never question me before." With Dan trying to gain my faith in him again, I told him that we can talk about it once we leave the deli. I was not going to have this discussion there in a public restaurant.

Once I got back to the table, I asked Timmy if we had an understanding. With a nod signaling yes, I left thirty dollars to cover everyone's coffee and food and tip. As everyone started to speak to me, I walked out the door and towards my truck. When I got half way to my truck, Dan came out the door behind me and yelled at me.

I stopped against my better judgment and turned to Dan. "Why do you want to push the issue? What do you have to gain?" While he was trying to figure out what to say, I finished walking to my truck when I felt Dan place his hand on my upper back. I turned back to him and as my eyes met his, Dan said; "We have been through a lot and I don't know what you're upset about."

I was provoked from Dan's actions since he was right about us being through a lot. I lost my temper and raised my voice this time. "Dan, you are a dirty whore. You're right that we have been through a lot, but you have recently been trying to go around me. My people are watching out to not be attacked. If one of them change sides, it is their call; but if they leave, they lose my trust. They will have to accept the consequences of their decision.

We are at war with the Himlee brothers because you wanted to cut me out of a deal that I said was bad the night before. You keep trying to use my name to get more than what I promised. Now you are going to Ferris telling him of my business. The two reasons I don't treat you like a whore and throw you on the street is because of all we have been through. You can keep being Ferris's guy, but don't expect me to be there any more than I would be for any other of my guys." I got in my truck. Before I drove off, I told Dan that he could give Ferris a ride since he has chosen to make deals with him and screw me.

I drove off without another thought about Dan's betrayal. Without paying much thought to the roads I was driving down, I realized that I was half a mile from my family's house. With being so close and not seeing my mom all week, I decided to stop by for a short visit. I started to drive down their driveway and saw my parents sitting on the patio with a few neighbors.

By the time I turned my truck off and got out, Paul had already walked up to me and told me to give him a hand grabbing some meat for the grill. Without a thought of why Paul wanted me to help carry some food, I followed him into the house. When the door closed behind me with just the sound of it latching, Paul handed me a stack of steaks. Then he began to tell me what was on his mind.

"So you know, I have been hearing things from people around the area. What I heard today has me concerned. Are you about to go too far with some kind of crap you're involved in? If you go to jail or get killed, I don't know what your mom will do. You are smart and you could do a lot of other things. This crap I hear you do is not going to allow you to have a real future. You also know that I just want the best for you."

All I could do after Paul said this to me was to promise him that I will do everything I can to stay safe. With that being said, we walked out of the house. Again with the door closing behind me, Paul told me to grab one more thing. Luckily, the last item I grabbed was a gallon jug of homemade wine.

Let me tell you, that the homemade wine I grew up drinking was the best wine I have ever tasted. I sometimes think back to when I would sit with a glass of wine on my mom's & Paul's porch and talk with my family. Those were good years and the memories made have stayed with me from the first sip.

After an hour with my family, I grabbed a bottle of wine and went home to Rose. When I got home, the place was empty. As it seemed odd to have my place to myself, I welcomed the time to sit down and have some time to sit in peace. I had to guess that it was about two in the afternoon and the sun was shining through the windows.

While I sat in my chair listening to some music and having a glass of wine, I got a phone call from Rose. She said that she was at Jenny's and she was being followed by a couple of guys. She already called Duke and he was on his way. I told her that I was on my way too. I followed up with telling her to stay inside the house.

Not thinking about the town that Rose was in, I put my wine in a travel mug and walked back to my truck. As I drove through the town of Gibsonburg, I saw the car Rose told me that was following her.

I drove by to see three guys sitting in the car. I turned the corner and parked my truck to take a little walk with my crowbar. I am not sure how I looked with a travel mug full of wine in one hand and a crowbar in the other hand. It was odd enough to have the local police stop to talk to me.

These cops were not friends of mine, but they knew me through my last name. One of the cops asked me if Cameron was my father and I told him that was according to my birth certificate. Cameron was not someone I considered to be family. The cop laughed and told me how he thought that Cameron was an asshole back when they were in school together. Then they asked what the crowbar was for. The only thing I could think to say was that I was lending it to a buddy. I don't know if they really did not care or what the reasoning was, but they drove off and I walked up around the corner and up the block. After walking up behind the car that had been following Rose around, I knocked on the driver side window. It took a moment for the guy behind the wheel to realize who I was. Then it all started.

Chapter Six

As fast as the guy driving could, he reached for the key to try to drive away. Being an old beat up car, it did not start right away. I did not wait for them to try again. I opened the door and pulled the driver out of the car. As he laid on the ground, I hit him in the knees with my crowbar. The other two guys got out to fight and I put my cup on the roof of their car.

I did not expect things to go smoothly for me with it being two to one. With that in mind; I went to hit one of the guys, but was punched in the back first. As the guy I was about to hit, kicked me in the ribs, I heard an old friend's voice.

This friend was crazy and love to fight. I knew it was my friend Tony as he yelled a line from an old movie called Goonies, he yells "Hey you Guys" and tackles the two guys. That gave me enough time to get back up to my feet and get back in the fight. The first thing I did was start attacking one of guys. I broke the guy's nose and with two open hands, I smacked both ears at the same time. He did not know where he was after that for a bit.

Tony, by the way, was punching the other guy on the ground and the guy I hit in the knee with the crowbar was crawling away. So, I grabbed my crowbar and went to town. This time hitting the kidney of the guy crawling. I guess I felt he was not hurt enough. Then the guy I was fighting came back to his senses. I did not want to let him get a chance to get back to his feet and fight again. So I hit him in the back of the ribs and a few kicks. Sadly, Tony knocked out the guy he was fighting with. I guess two out of three were enough to listen to what I had to say would still work. As long as my message got back to Mark and Jay.

I began to tell the two who were still conscious, that I am not going to hurt them anymore. That is unless they did something to cause me to feel as if I needed to. You would think that I would be angry with them for following Rose. I expected to have to hold myself back from doing something worst, but that was not the case. I was well aware that these guys were doing what they were told to do. I was, in fact, angry with the Himlee brothers and I was happy thinking about addressing part of my issue shortly. So back to these guys.

With a clear mind and a few new bruises, I told the two guys still awake that they were going to give Mark and Jay some advice for me. I basically said, "They should learn to sleep with one eye open and never be alone. Mark and Jay will learn messing with my girl is an unforgivable mistake. I will keep my end of the agreement and not involve anyone who is not involved. But remind Mark and Jay they have involved most of their family. I protect mine and keep them out of my business." With that being said; Tony and I loaded them back into their car. As I started to walk away, Tony being the smart ass that he was, told them to drive safely and then whispered in the ear of the guy sitting in the driver seat and grabbed my travel mug off of the roof for me. I don't know what Tony said and never asked. I do know that the guy looked scared and promised Tony he would not ever come back. I would honestly hate to image what Tony had said. Tony was a friend of mine, so I knew him well enough to know that he could put chills down someone's spine.

The good thing about Tony, if you're a friend of his, he would not think twice to take a punch for you. You just better be willing to do the same or you will not be on his good side. In fact, it was because of this, Tony and I became friends.

It was probably two years before when I saw two guys kicking him while he was on the ground. I stopped my car and ran to help him. This was also when I realized how much I liked my crowbar. Because when I hit one guy across his shoulder blades, he fell like a rock. His other friend took off leaving the guy on the ground next to Tony.

I am not sure why I stopped to help Tony. He was a guy who I saw around but never spoke to much before that day. That was also the same question Tony asked when he got to his feet. I could only make jokes like, "I could not let you have all the fun" and other random B.S. that he just chuckled about. The only reason I helped was that I could not stand seeing an unfair fight.

From that day, Tony and I were friends. We were not close friends, but we talked when we saw each other and we would stand up for each other if it was needed. I find it funny that Duke became good friends with Tony. They were completely different, but Duke was able to become friends with about anyone.

So it was not too much of a surprise when Duke showed up in his car and started talking to both of us. Once Duke was no longer concerned about us, he invited Tony to come into Jenny's house. Since it was only half a block away and I think Tony had a thing for Duke's girlfriend, Tony joined us. I don't think that Duke knew how Tony felt either. As we walked, Tony smelled what was in my travel mug and said to me, "This must be yours." He handed it to me and asked why I brought wine with me to a fight. I laughed and said that there is never a bad time to have homemade wine.

The three of us ended up on the porch of a white house and sitting on the swing. Meanwhile, Duke was knocking on the door. While Tony and I sat down, he asked what the fight was over. Funny that he did not care to ask sooner, but that was my type of friends. Ready to jump in, but not worry about the why till later. I started to tell Tony what was going on and got halfway through when the door opened and the girls came out. First Duke's girl Jenny came through the door, then Rose, but you would think that they were trying to get out at the same time.

Before we got a word out, they started telling us their story about being followed and the danger they felt. Listening to them, they were dodging bullets and jumping out of the way of speeding cars. But they were safe and that is really all I cared about. The fact that I was bleeding from a cut on my cheek, was not noticed until Rose went to kiss me when their story was done.

It was not a big cut, more of a scratch, but still had some blood coming out of it. So, we went into the house and got cleaned up. Rose started to ask what happened and where the guys following them went to. Rose was stalked by a guy a while back, which is why she kept a close watch if someone was following her. So things like this put her on edge and reminded her of the last time she was followed by her ex-boyfriend who did not want to let go. But when I caught up with him, he was informed that his actions were bad for his physical health. That was a a little over a year ago.

This day; Tony, Duke, and I were inside cleaning up inside Jenny's parents' house. I must say that her house gave me the creeps. They were remodeling and taking down the old slat walls to put up good insulation and drywall. They had recently got the plaster off and you could see the thin boards going across the studs. It put me in mind of a scary movie house. You know, where the sun just finds a bit of an opening in the window and you see the dust drafting by.

As I sat down on a plastic covered chair, Jenny came out of the kitchen and handed Rose a bowl full of water with a washcloth. Rose jokingly said, "Did you chase off those bad guys for little ole me?" and she started to smile at me. When I went to make a smart ass comment, Tony jumped in and said that he helped. Duke told Tony thanks for helping keep the girls safe. Rose leaned close to me while wiping my face and said that I will get thanked later. Rose and Jenny giggled, then went into the kitchen while us guys just sat in the creepy Living room.

We sat there quietly for about a minute when Tony stood up to go and said that we can give his number to both girls. He was not going to get involved with what was going on between the Himlee's and me, but he would watch out for them. They could also come to his place if they need a safe place. Then Tony was out the door and back on his way to where ever he was going, when he stopped to help me.

Rose suggested we go swimming and have a break. We decided to go to an old small stone quarry that was filled with water where we used to swim in it during the summers. This was a great place when I was a kid. The quarry was wrapped with trees and bushes that hide it from everything outside. It was also set far enough back that no one would notice a little campfire at night. Some of my favorite memories included hanging out there. This day at the quarry was a good memory because I knew it could have been my last time there.

As Duke, Jenny, Rose and I were swimming, we heard someone coming back. This has a few reasons I was nervous about who it could be. If it was a cop, we could be arrested for trespassing and I had a gun with me. The quarry was on private property and the owner did not like us being back there.

If it was someone that had a grudge with me or one of Himlee's guys; I was out of reach of my gun. I did not watch if we were followed or if someone had seen my truck. After everything that happened in the past few days, I could not count it out. The funny thing is a few years ago, Mark and a small group of us would go to that quarry. We would drink, smoke weed, and just bullshit. This was back when Mark and I worked for the same guy.

Finally, it could be someone trying to be stupid and would start trouble since everyone in Risingsun and the small towns around us knew of this quarry. There were all kinds of people that would come back. Most times it would be someone that would be easy to hang out with or kept to themselves. Every now and again people who like to start fights or want to be flat out asses will come back.

Instead of waiting for whoever it was to get back to us, I told everyone to hide under a little overhang. As they listened and hid, I swam towards our stuff. Just when I got out of the water, a breeze hit my back and gave me a chill. That stopped me for a moment, but I got moving again and grabbed my pants. Before I was able to get my gun out of its holster, I saw Riggs and his girlfriend walking around the corner. When he yelled over to me, everyone else came out and we got back to enjoying ourselves.

I don't know how Riggs knew we were back there, but I guess one of the girls must have called before we left. It was a good ending of the day considering how the day went earlier.

When we decided to call it and go back to our cars, Rose told me she was staying with Jenny that night. I think she said they were going to some show the next day. She might have told me about this and I forgot, but I did not want to point that out. I smiled and told her to have fun, then gave her a kiss and got in my truck. She got in Duke's car with Jenny and Duke. That is when I decided to go get dinner in Fostoria before going home.

Chapter Seven

I had a good dinner and the night with no plans. It was getting dark and most the people I know are going to sleep. Either they had to work or had gotten high. I did have a friend who didn't do drugs and might have been home and awake. I took a chance to see if I could hang out.

I never made it to his door though. I pulled up to the house he rented and as I was about to get out of my truck, I saw Jay Himlee walking along the road. Considering everything going on, this must be the dumbest thing he could do.

He had to have walked out of a place where he was getting high or drunk and a lot. Jay was not walking right and he was covered in mud. I figured he had fallen down or been pushed down. With how he stumbled, I would of bet that he fell on his own.

Without a thought, I grabbed my gun and walked up behind him. I lifted my clean and cold gun to the back of his ear. I wanted him to feel the cold metal and know he was not getting out of this.

I thought about pulling the trigger right there and leave his body in the gutter, but that was too good for him. But hitting him with the gun felt really good and he fell to the ground.

It hurt him enough, but I think him being drunk or high was what really knocked him out. If a strong breeze hit Jay, he would have fallen over and been out. Either way, he was unconscious and I was not going to wait for him to wake up.

I got my truck and pulled it over to where Jay laid on the

ground. I started wrapping him up with a blue tarp and rope that I kept in my truck. Jay did not looked as he was no more than hundred and ten pounds, but moving over to the truck, I would have guessed that he was around one–fifty if not more. It was good that I was young and in good shape.

With some effort, I put the jack ass in the bed of my truck. As Jay was laying there, I put another tarp over him and tied it down as if I was hauling a bale of straw. I drove up a few blocks to a pay phone next to a seven–eleven and called Mick. It was time for him to get his payback as I promised. I told him where we needed to meet and to bring the girl with him. Just don't do anything to her till we talked in person. After Mick agreed and hung up the phone, I got back in my truck and drove off.

Now, this was not what I planned for Jay, but at that moment, I could kill two birds with one stone. The plan I had would go out the window. I was planning to have Jay thrown in one of the holes that the guy who owed me money was going to dig. It was a very detailed plan, but the end results were to bury him alive and have a pipe coming up to provide him some air. I would have made it last as long as I could. After three days of no food or water in the summer heat, I would pour gas down the tube and lite it up. The best part was that I was going to have the girl who stabbed Mick, killed and left on Jay's bedroom floor.

I don't believe that the holes were dug. I wanted to give Mick revenge on both Jay and that girl that attacked him as quick as I can. So, I came up with a new plan. I would not wait for another chance. While Jay was tied up and laid in the bed of my truck, I drove to a small "lake" called Mosier Lake that was just outside of Fostoria. There was a nice space out of site just a short drive half way back off of Independence Avenue. This area was not well known at the time and that is where I waited for Mick.

It did not take long after I got there, Jay started talking and not using the nicest of words. When Jay calmed down, he started to ask questions as if he believed he was in control of what was going on. I had not even uncovered him so Jay could not see anything other than the blue of my tarp and truck bed. I could only laugh at him as I got a few things out of my toolbox. I wanted to be ready to get everything done when Mick arrived. I wanted to be as quick as I could. I hated staying around an area that I knew could end me up behind bars.

I was lucky that the moon was out and there was enough light to see what I was doing. I did not have to turn on any lights and could see clearly. I opened my center console when I noticed the contact information that James gave me and I put it in my pocket. I went back on my way and noticed a car coming down the gravel road that led back to the clearing that I was sitting in.

I slipped my gun into the back of my pants and got ready for anything. Considering that I had Jay in my truck bed, I am sure that a cop would not be as understanding as I would hope. If my luck held out, it was a couple trying to find a private place to get off.

In fact, that is how I knew of this place. I used to go there when I dated the girl before Rose. I loved the things that girl did, but she is no longer around. I still wonder whatever happened to her. I believed she could have done anything she put her mind to. Then one day, she was gone without a word. When I went to her house, it was empty except for a few dust bunnies.

Now back to the car coming down the road. I noticed that the car was a maroon Mercury Marquis. That is what Mick drove and he always said he joked about how many bodies he could fit in the trunk. I don't know how Mick got to me so quickly. He had to run from his house to go get that girl who attacked him and then drive to me. This was at least a 45-minute trip and that is if he was driving normally. I guess he must have had wings on his car, because it took him much less than that to get there.

Mick pulled up next to my truck and got out of his car holding a rope with a noose at one end. He held it up and said, "We are doing it my way". As I was about to ask what he had planned, Mick asked me what Church the Himlee's belong to. Not sure what Church had to do with what we were doing, I was only thinking about what I planned would have been simple. I would have the girl kill Jay and shot her up with a strong dose of heroin to kill her in an overdose. I figured it would look like a drug deal gone wrong.

Mick did not wait for me to reply and said that Jay is Catholic. Saying "His family goes to the same church as my Aunt. At least the ones that are not strung out still went. Their church has a strict rule not allowing any suicide person to have last rites or a proper Catholic funeral". This made Mick laugh and he gave me a creepy feeling. I understood what Mick was saying and how he was planning to hurt Jay and his family in death as well.

The Himlee family used to be big into the Catholic Church and Mick's Aunt had told him how snobbish they were about it. Mick knew that Mark would not only feel the pain of his brother's death, but the pain would have forced Mark to think his brother will never be in heaven. I did not think this mattered as I had given up on religion.

I walked to my truck and got Jay from it. Mick walked over to one of the trees at the back of our location. By the time I threw Jay on the ground and started removing the ropes, Mick was standing next to me. He was holding a gun ready in case Jay tried anything. Once Jay had realized where he was and who he was with, he started to cry and plead for us to let him go.

It must have been close to ten at night by the time Jay shut up and stood up. I pulled my gun out and lead him to one of the big rocks sticking out of the ground and told him to sit. Jay had become a different person and acted like a child being scolded for breaking a window by his mom. I honestly was surprised as Jay did not try to make threats or try to fight his way to be free.

Instead, Jay sat on the rock with his head hung low and his hands tucked in his armpits. I did not let this bother me and remembered what Jay has had others do for him. I now realized why he had others do everything for him. How pathetic he was. Jay would end his life as a 16-year-old High School dropout and only was pretending to be a tough thug.

I told Jay that I would not kill him, that is if he does what we tell him. Before I was even able to continue and tell Jay what he had to do, he agreed to do anything. Mick started to tell Jay what he had to do. It all sounded simple and I did not see where Mick was going with all of this, whatever it was he was doing. Mick had a smile on his face from ear to ear.

Mick told Jay that he had to have sex with the girl that was meant to stab me but got him instead. Once Jay was finished, he was to turn the girl around and stab her in the chest until she was dead. Then he was done and he could get dressed. Mick did tell him that the girl told him that she had some STD, but did not tell him which one. Without another word, Mick went to his car and opened the trunk.

You could tell the girl was high when Mick pulled her out of his trunk. He must have given her something before putting her in the truck. Mick started to pull her by her hair and halfway between his car and Jay. Then he stopped and you could see he whispered something in her ear and she nodded her head. Not a moment later, Mick started walking again with her in tow. I thought that Mick would have dragged her through the gravel if she would have fallen.

I don't know why, but when Mick let go of the girl and she fell to the ground, I wondered what her name was. Not once have I asked or even cared. Now that I was about to watch her die, I started to wonder what it says about me that this did not bother me. But I got it out of my own head and said: "let's get this all done."

Jay got up and picked her up, then told her that he would be quick with everything. I sat down on my tailgate while Mick stood within a few arm's lengths of them. Mick wanted to make sure that everything went the way he wanted it to. Jay stripped her and pushed her over the rock he sat on. He dropped his pants and tried to start, but Jay was not able to get it up to do anything.

I don't know why, but I could not help to laugh when Jay and the girl started to both cry. This must have only gone on for about a minute, but I laughed for a while. When I composed myself, the girl had turned around and was giving Jay a blowjob to help him get up. I could only imagine Mick told her to have sex with Jay and he would not hurt her. Once Jay calmed down, he got into it and the girl turned back around to let Jay do what he had to do.

65

After about five minutes, Jay started making noises and I guessed that it was what Jay did when he got off. Mick cleared his throat to let Jay know that he was not done. Jay turned her around and was looking at each other in the eyes. I did hear Jay ask her what STD she had. I started to laugh again when she said AIDS. Jay got a look on his face that was a mixture of fear and anger. Mick handed Jay a knife and Jay started to stab her till her chest and stomach was destroyed.

Jay fell to the ground crying again. His pants around his ankle, his bare knees on the graveled ground, and a dead naked drug addict girl laid in front of him. Without waiting Mick helped Jay up and told him to pull up his pants.

Once Jay had his pants up, Jay had been walked over to the tree where Mick put up the noose. I had to think Jay was not paying close attention to anything as he did not react to the rope with a noose. Jay did not do anything when Mick helped him onto some stones that were meant to be a platform. As Jay stood on the stones, Mick quickly put the noose around Jay's neck and jumped back. When Mick jumped off the stones, they slid around and no longer supported Jay. With the stones gone, there was about a two-foot gap between Jay and the ground.

I never have seen someone hung. I had heard that back in the days' people use to hang people for crimes, it could take a while for the person to die. Jay did not take long as soon as the stones were gone, he shook for a few minutes and then went limp. His body was swinging there and I questioned if Jay wanted to die after the girl told him that she had AIDS. It could also be the shock of seeing blood on his hands and knowing he had killed someone. Either way, Jay Himlee would not be causing me any more problems.

Mick stood there looking at Jay swinging at the end of the rope. I had no clue what Mick was thinking as he watched. When I looked at Jay, I noticed that one hand had the girl's blood on it. There was not a lot of blood, but enough that I realized that the rope should have some too. So I went over to the girl as she laid after grabbing some rawhide gloves from my truck. Once I had them on, I made a fist and as if I was holding the knife myself, I started to push my hand onto the blood soaked shirt that she wore. There was a lot of blood, but I only needed enough to put some blood on the rope. With enough blood covering my thumb and pointer finger, I went to the rope that Jay was hanging from. I started to grab the rope as I figured Jay would have to put the rope around his neck and to tie it to the tree.

Mick started talking as if he thought he was talking the whole time. He said "Well?" and I was confused, it had to show on my face too. I think what he said next was what he thought he said. "Why are you putting the girl's blood on the rope?" I pointed to Jay's hand and asked if he sees the blood on his hand. Mick said "Yeah", and I asked how did he put the rope up and around his neck without getting any blood on it. Then I saw on Mick's face that he understood what I was saying and he was nodding his head up and down. I just was content that it was done and so was Jay.

Now I needed to deal with Mark Himlee. I didn't think Mark would accept that his brother committed suicide. My only concern of Mark was that I did not know how far he would go. As I said before, Mark was not a big fan of Violence. He only had someone do something when there was no other option. I saw Mark fight once. There was a reason Mark did not fight and that is why he had others fight for him.

I believed that people would do what Mark wanted because they were afraid of what Jay would do. Jay always acted as though he was the type of guy who would go crazy over stupid stuff. People did not know how to deal with that, but I saw that Jay was all talk and nothing more than a scared kid. Now Jay was gone and if there is a Hell, he would spend eternity there.

Mick walked over to me and asked if there was anything left. I asked him if he could go find Jay's friend Timmy. I told Mick "tell Timmy that he watched Jay lose his mind after screwing some girl. Jay had gotten rough with her and when Jay finished with her, she told him that she had AIDS. After Jay stabbed her, he hung himself. Then tell Timmy that he left to find the police to have them help him." Mick started to laugh and walked away. I don't know how, but I heard that around 1:00am, Timmy was at the police station leading them to the opening at Mosier Lake.

I heard that as the police walked around, Timmy had broken down in tears. He knew to stick to his story after seeing what happened to Jay. I think Timmy had been scared of what would happen if he stops telling the same story to anyone who asked. I heard that Timmy got into drugs too much and overdosed. I was content that he served his purpose that day and I did not have to deal with him ever again.

Chapter Eight

I don't know what time it was, but the sun was shining through my windows and I was still in bed. After a long night and seeing all that I did, I was exhausted. I was woken by a lot of knocking on my door. I felt if I did not get up and answer the door, whoever was on the other side would have knocked till the door fell down.

When I got to the door, I saw the curtain open on the door and Riggs standing there waiting for me. He was looking around and acting like he was scared of something. When I opened the door, Riggs walked in and asked me if I heard about Jay Himlee.

For fun, I acted like I knew nothing about it and wanted to see what he had to say. I asked what he was talking about. I insisted he tell me what he heard. He went off telling me about how Jay killed himself after he killed some girl. Then he asked if the girl we were keeping at the house got free or did we let her go. I guess he heard it was the same girl who stabbed Mick was the same one Jay killed.

I told Riggs that she must have gotten free and ran back to Jay. With a smile, I also said "this is one less problem I will have to worry about. Now I have to deal with Mark and anyone else that gets in my way."

Riggs kept looking at me till I asked him why he was at my place that early. He said that he thought I was planning to kill Jay and it seems odd that he did it himself. Then he went back sitting quietly and staring at me.

I did not say anything, because I knew what he was getting at and I wanted to keep as few people in the loop as I could. This was because people like to whisper about what they know and act as though they are special to have info. Then when someone gets in trouble, they will use that information to save their own ass.

So Riggs let the question of my involvement go and kept talking about what everyone is saying. It's interesting that most of the information is coming from Timmy. Timmy kept telling everyone the story that Mick told him to use. I almost thought he told so many people, so quick, is so he could memorize the story.

I knew that some would think I killed Jay, but Timmy was the biggest tool to quiet any thoughts others had. This was clear when Riggs handed me a newspaper from that morning. The cover story had a big headline in bold saying "DRUGS FUELED MURDER/SUICIDE".

With my interest getting the best of me, I pick up the paper to read the story. I was expecting a story about Jay and some details that the police had. I quickly realized that was not the case. The writer must have not talked with anyone and heard about what happened over the police radio.

As I read the paper, it talked about how the youth in the communities are all on drugs. Then how Jay Himlee was a young man who got some drugs and killed himself after killing the girl. The story was more of a public service message about drugs, than a story about what happened.

The article was a bunch of rumors, hearsay, and the writer's opinion. By the time I put the paper down, Riggs was pulling food from my fridge. I never understood why everyone thought they could get into anything I had in my home. At least they all stayed out of my bedroom or did not walk into my house uninvited.

Riggs sat back down and ate whatever it was he grabbed. Riggs started talking again. This time about a party he heard about and how he was taking his girlfriend to it. I stopped listening to him while I got dressed. Then looked to see if there was any food to eat.

All I had was some potatoes, cheese, ranch dressing, and

lunch meat. I guess I get to make a baked potato. Don't get me wrong, I like my baked potatoes. I load them up to where it is a meal itself. I don't like my frig to be empty, but I had not been grocery shopping and Riggs was eating my last leftovers.

I looked over to Riggs as he was walking to the kitchen with an empty plate. When he placed the plate in my sink, he started to mumble something. His body was drooping as though he was doing everything he could to hold himself up. He also was acting as if he did not want to look at me.

Not a clue to what he said, I asked him to repeat himself without whatever he had in his mouth, and to clean his plate. I thought I was being funny, but Riggs hung his head low and told me his personal news. This was the real reason he came over.

Riggs said that he promised his mom that he was going to sign up for the military after he stopped by a few places. Then he finished his news by telling me that he would not be hanging out with me, Dan, or Duke. He was going to spend as much time as he could with his family and girlfriend before boot camp.

I understood that he needed to do what he needed to. I smiled at him and wished him luck. Finally, I opened the front door and gave him a big hug as he walked out my door. Then he was gone before I knew it. That was the last time I saw him. As he said, after leaving my place, Riggs signed up for the Marines.

After thinking of the events, I finished getting myself around and went out to find a few people. It would have been good to stay in and let everything from the previous night process, but I didn't have time. There were things I had to get in order. I was worried about what Mark might do. I had no idea at that time how he would take his brother's death.

I did not think Mark would believe his brother killed himself. That meant that he would most likely blame me. I hoped that he kept to our agreement and would leave anyone not in the business out of our fight. He has been a man of his word as long as I have known him. With that in mind and my jeans back on, I headed out the door.

While driving down route 6 and coming up to US 23, I

stopped at fuel mart to fill up. That is when I saw Mick's car sitting in the Subway restaurant attached to the gas station. So I went in and sat with him to see how he was doing.

Mick looked lost in his thoughts. As I sat there, he just stared at me. I guessed he had to be processing what happened. Mick had never watched someone die. The worst Mick had seen or had been involved with was the beating of a guy who ended up with broken bones. In fact, he put a guy in the hospital, but never took a life.

"How are you holding up? I know last night was your first time." I was not too worried about talking to Mick. This was because no one was around except for a guy behind the counter that was stoned, and he would not know anything. He most likely did not even know he was at work.

I pulled out a cigarette and lit it and offered Mick one. He waved his hand to turn down my offer. Mick said with a far off look on his face, "I don't know how I did that. I don't know how it still doesn't bother me. I am scared of myself and now I know what I am able to do to someone."

We kept sitting in the booth for a bit without talking. I reached in my pocket and pulled out that James's guy's information and handed it to Mick. With a smile, as Mick takes the paper, I said "I think this James guy will be good for something in the future. Don't worry about him either. He owes us enough money. I already told him that I have something for him to do and even his tab. And Mick, you know you are able to protect yourself or anyone you want to. Don't think about it as a bad thing."

Mick stood up and walked out. I still needed to fill my trucks tan, so I walked over to the convenient store register to give twenty dollars to the clerk. I pointed to my truck and he nods to me. I guess these people are not talkative or they all were on something. I was OK with both options; I needed gas and not conversation.

Once I had my gas, I got back on the road and drove until I found myself at the house. Ferris came out when I pulled into the drive. He was still dressed like a guy from the city and looked out of place. I think he tried to dress how he thought country people dressed. At best, he would have been called an urban cowboy. In the short time he was there, people got a good laugh about his clothing choices.

His clothes had nothing to do with what he was doing or my thoughts of him, but it did not help him either. When I got out of my truck, Ferries walked up to me in the grass. He was avoiding getting his shoes dirty in the dirt driveway. He said that we need to talk, and he didn't know what I would think.

"Ok, let's go sit on the porch. It's a nice day and I would like to have something to enjoy as you discuss whatever you had on your mind." After saying this, I realized how dumb it sounded, but Ferris didn't make any comments. I let Ferris take the first seat on the porch. By the time my butt hit the seat, he started to talk.

He told me of his plan to leave Ohio and go back to New York City. He spoke with his boss John and made arrangements to get a ride with a guy that is driving through with the product.

Ferris seemed to have a need to tell me why he was leaving and some touchy–feely crap. But he pissed me off when he said that Dan agreed to give him a ride to meet with the guy driving through. This pissed me off because I saw this as another attempt for Dan to try and go around me. Dan knew I had started developing a relationship with the drivers during the exchanges. They help me get out from under Deatz and build what I had.

I most likely would have shot Dan in the face if he was there. Instead I told Ferris that he will get a ride with Mick. I angrily continued telling Ferris that Mick is my second in command. Dan is someone trying to get into something he knows nothing about and will get himself killed. Plus, Mick could make an exchange for product and disburse it.

With the look on Ferris's face, I thought he was a little scared of me at that moment. He tried to act like he was fearless, but you learn what fear in someone's eyes look like. For Ferris, he knew he was on his own and I figured he was always surrounded by his people before he came to Ohio.

The simple response Ferris gave me was that he would do

what I told him. I knew from then he would not involve Dan in anything to do with business. I thought Dan and I were on the same page, but this is a reminder that I can't trust him.

Everything Ferris told me; I learned a guy would be coming threw for an unscheduled stop. This meant I did not have time to find Dan if I wanted to try and buy whatever the guy had.   It seemed that I had to push back dealing with Dan if I could get the time.

Now I had to reach out to John and see what I could buy and if he wants cash or counterfeit money or a mixture. I believed there was about five thousand dollars' worth in ten–dollar bills. There should also have been five thousand dollars' worth of twenties too. The counterfeit money was mad for John. I would let it sit till he had a desire for them. I did this because I made an agreement with John that he got everything we made and I got my products at a discount.

In about an hour I was standing by a pay phone waiting for a call. It was never a direct call to John. First, I had to call a pager of a person who called me and gave my message to John. It was rare to have John call to talk to me. He worried that the police or Feds would be listening to him. So it shocked me when he returned my call.

When the pay phone rang, I answered it with my normal greeting of "Hello from 419" and waited for the response. Then I heard John say "212 here and enjoying the sights." We talked for about fifteen minutes after that. We used a lot of code in our conversation and I didn't think that anyone would have a problem breaking the code. We used vegetables and livestock in place of certain drugs and any other illegal stuff.

I found out that John also ran some legal retail businesses. It was a good way to launder money and have a cover. If someone tried to ask about his phone calls, he used one of his stores' needs as an excuse. That seemed to be smart to me. I didn't have the size of operation he had. I ran a small brokerage company and did manage some farmers. I was not getting rich with it, but I made some money to show an income.

By the end of talking with John, we had an agreement. Now I had to go find Duke for my real and counterfeit money. I never asked Ferris when he was leaving, but John told me I had two days to make the exchange. I was purchasing everything the guy was carrying. It cost me all the counterfeit money I had and another twenty grand in real cash. This would be my biggest deal at one time. I was kind of excited to see everything.

I found Duke at Jenny's house after calling around for about an hour. Once I knew where he was, I tried to get there as soon as I could. He was waiting for the girls to come back. I was excited to see him when I got there.

After Riggs visit, Ferris's talk, and making this deal with John, I felt exhausted. My plan was to tell Duke what I needed him to put together and ask him to give it to Mick. After that, I would sit with Duke and talk while waiting and that is what I did.

An hour and a half passed when the girls pulled up. I was able to tell Duke everything that I needed him to do and what all happened, so we were able to have time for the girls. Duke did give some advice that helps me relax and remember why I am doing this all.

The girls were high on excitement and looked tired at the same time. As they got out of the car, they came over to us and they both began telling us about the adventure they had. I don't know about Duke, but I didn't catch most of what they said. When those two girls talked at the same time, I normally only caught a quarter of it.

It was OK that I didn't hear everything. I knew that they had fun and were safe. That was all I needed to know. By the time they finished talking, Rose asked if I would take her home. I told her I would and we can just relax for the rest of the evening. She then said no and corrected my thinking by saying she meant her home. She had to go to her mom's house and that is where her address was. So I nodded to say yes and she gave me a big kiss.

It was nice to have time with Rose, Duke, and Jenny. We spent about two hours talking and telling jokes. That was, till the girls started to yawn. So, I took Rose back to her mom's house and went to my place.

When I got home and inside, I saw a message on my machine. I walked by it without touching it. At that time, I did not have an urge to hear any possible bad news. So I first got a beer from the fridge and ordered a pizza. Back then, I used to love a good taco pizza.

Once I was done stalling, I listened to the message. It was Duke telling me that he got a hold of Mick and they set up a time to meet the next day. He said Mick wants me to call him after 8:00 to talk. Then the machine let me know that there are no more messages.

For a while, I enjoyed the silence. No TV or people talking to fill the space. I turned on the radio to some classical music for background music. I even got excited that I would have time to read. I grabbed my copy of Dante's Inferno and opened it to where my bookmark was. This was my third time reading this copy, so I had notes written in the empty areas of the pages. I like to make notes with questions or things I learned about the book.

I had finished reading another five pages when my phone started to ring. The phone was across the room and I didn't want to get up. Sadly, I did not have a choice. I am not sure who was calling or if it would be an emergency. I only knew that I had too much going on to miss a call.

Crossing my fingers that it was Rose wanting to see if she could come over, I answered the phone, but I am not that lucky. When I picked up the phone, I heard Mick. He was frantic about not knowing what was going on and he wanted to come over right then.

After trying to calm Mick down, he told me that he was grabbing his keys and heading over to see me. I stopped him and asked him to wait until the morning. When he asked why, I indicated that I was working on something and I needed time to finish it.

He stalled before he agreed with me, but he got there and said OK. I finished up our conversation by telling him that my door will be unlocked for him to come in. I got back to my project of enjoying a quiet night and my book. I am glad that none of my guys question me too much.

They may ask a general question or try to figure more out than what I tell them, but they all smile and nod in the end. This why that night I got to sit and read. No fighting, no one to give orders to, and no friends I had to explain what was happening. That night was a night of beer, pizza, and my book to clear my head. That was, till I fell asleep on the chair.

Chapter Nine

The sun must have just broken above the ground. That is when I got woken up to Mick walking around my kitchen making a pot of coffee. Mick was looking at me while I was asleep in my chair as my eyes opened and he says, "I told you I would be here first thing."

Mick was one to do what he says. I figured that Mick meant that he would be at my place around 9:00, but instead, I can see the clock read 6:15am. What 20-year old that makes a living by helping run a business like ours is up that early? Most of our people work late in the night meeting "Johns", selling drugs, or whatever else I gave them to sell.

Mick was the guy who collected money from the lower level guys and sold the guns with me. Now I am having him make a product exchange. This was something that would take him a few minutes to learn and could do it over a cup of coffee. But while the coffee was brewing, I went and got myself around. Even though it seems people stopping by my place tends to see me in my PJ's or boxers. I prefer that I had my jeans or good pants on when talking this time, but I fell asleep wearing what I wore all day.

In a short time, I was back out with a clean pair of pants and shirt on. As I walked out to the living room, Mick was changing the station on my radio. He most likely did not like the relaxed mood or the classical music station. Other than noticing Mick playing with the radio, I did not pay any attention to anything other than getting a cup of coffee. I saw the full pot waiting for me and my empty cup sitting next to it. I had not gotten the sleep out of my eye and a cup or two of coffee should help me focus more. Once I got my first cup of coffee, I turned around to see Mick holding out his hand for a cup of coffee. The bastard got my coffee and I got another cup for myself out of the cabinet and filled it up.

Now that I had my coffee, I was ready to talk with Mick and I joined him at my kitchen island. Mick did not even wait for my ass to hit the seat when asking me why he had to meet with Duke. He even sounded like he got upset that Duke called him and he thought that he was getting an order. I got this when Mick started to rant. I don't know if the stress of everything is taking its toll on him or if he got upset because his pride got hurt. Either way, I listened to him get everything off his chest.

Mick said "Why is Duke calling me? We agreed that I only took orders from you and I take care of things to get the job done. You never questioned me before and now you are changing things. What has changed that you are putting Duke above me?" After some more things being said, none of which concerned me, he shut up. Now I had half my cup of coffee drank and was ready to explain what was going on. Mick looked at me as I put down my cup.

"Mick, you are still my right-hand man and somebody I trusted fully. You know that you are the one who is to take my place if anything happens to me. In fact, you are the only one who knows where I put my secret stashes and who gets what." With Mick's face blank, I kept talking. I told him "I asked Duke to reach out to you so he can meet with you and give you money and other stuff. You need this because I am having you take Ferris to meet with a guy tomorrow who will be taking him back to New York City. Ferris is leaving, but you will be taking everything Duke gives you and give it to the guy picking up Ferris. This will be the largest exchange I ever have done and I want you to handle it. This should also tell you that you are still my go to."

This got Mick to smile and he started nodding his head up and down. I think he wanted to do this for a bit. He kept talking about us being partners and him doing more so that I was not always stressed out. Now that Mick knew what I wanted him to do, his attitude had changed and he was full of energy. I guess I should have had Mick do more before and accepted him as a partner. Truth be told, I would not have been able to build what I did without Mick. He knew that if I left, went to prison, or got killed; he would be the one to take over.

So while he was as happy as he was, I told him that I can't have him keep working for me. With a smile on my face, I told him that he is my partner and we will have everything split fifty-fifty. I no longer wanted to worry that he was going to leave and start up his own little business or figure out how to get rid of me. After what we went through the other night, I knew that Mick was ready to do whatever was needed.

Let me say that Mick has never hugged me. Most he has done before is shake my hand, but he mostly nodded towards me. To say it simply, Mick was not normally an excitable man. That was till he heard my offer. He jumped up from his chair and lifted me up from my chair with a big hug. I lost my breath for a bit and I believed that some of my ribs were bruised. When he got over the excitement and his emotions back in check, he let go of me and we both sat back in our chairs.

I only could laugh till the pain got too much when he said that he thinks he will accept. Not that I had a question about it, but it was still good to hear. While he was grabbing his keys to go and also one of my coffee travel mugs, I told him to leave me some coffee, and anything that comes in today and forward is half his. He nodded and walked out of my door. I pictured he was smiling once he knew I could not see.

That day was not too exciting after Mick Left. I ran around getting things in line to deal with Mark Himlee and load up on more ammo. I wanted to have enough to shoot every one of Mark's guys twice if I needed. This is not to say that I went out looking for them. I did not want to have any more bloodshed and

I would prefer to let things go back to normal. What I wanted to do is turn over the drugs, girls, and counterfeiting to Mick when Rose goes to college. I plan to keep the gun running and grow that.

By the end of the day, I did not hear anyone say that Mark was out looking for me or saying anything about him coming after me. Not even a word of him being seen away from his family. I wanted to hedge my bet, that maybe, Mark did not think I was involved or did not plan to come after me. That is when I grabbed a bottle of Maker's Mark that I had and drove over to Mark's house.

Mark and Jay lived with their mother, but there were other family members living in that house too. I did not know who they were, I knew they had Mark or Jay sell them some drugs. Everyone, except Mark, would sit in the house getting high most of the day. When you would walk up to the house, you could see it had been nice place. It would have taken some work since the paint was peeling off all over to put it back in the original state.

Looking at the house, you could see the wood showing around the patches of blue paint. Then looking up to the second story, the windows were broken and had wood panels covering the openings. I know that Mark had money, but I could only imagine that he kept it hidden from everyone in that house. The house was run down and I expect that the inside did not look better than the outside. As I walked up on the porch, my foot went through the first step.

When I got to Mark's house and knocked on the door. A guy with red eyes and looking like he has not showered in weeks answered the door. If it was not for seeing Mark's car parked on the street, I would not have stopped. I never understood why Mark lived in his family house. He had to hide everything he had or let it get stolen. Everyone else in the house refused to work and did everything they could to collect welfare.

After about five minutes asking the guy if he could get Mark, Mark walked by and noticed me. Mark came over to talk with me and get that guy to go back to wherever he came from. So, Mark and I sat on his front porch with plenty of space between us. I don't know if Mark had a gun on him or close, but I had mine on me. I did not need it at the time, but I wanted to be safe.

After we both figured where we were going to sit, we started to talk. I could see that he was on edge with me being there. He was also dealing with Jay's death. I don't think anyone else in that house was sober enough to understand that Jay was dead. I started our conversation by saying that I understand he was dealing with a lot of pain. I also said that it is hard to deal with these feelings, family, and still trying to run a business. Before I could say anything more, Mark asked me what I wanted and why was I at his house. That is when I went to my truck and returned with the bottle of Maker's Mark. I handed it to him and watched him pull the red waxed pull tab to open the bottle. Mark took the cap off, smelled it, and then sat it back down. He still had not said anything, but got up and went in his house.

It was not long before he came back out with two coffee mugs and handed me one. Once I took the mug, he smiled and sat down. I blew some dust out of the mug and held it out. Mark poured some of the bourbon in my cup after he put it in his. It had been a long time since we had sat down together as two guys. This led us to talk about a lot of things that we only knew. We spoke about things we have seen with people doing drugs and the stupid things we heard from the guys we had selling for us. We even talked about what we used to say we would do when we got away from our small towns. We drank half the bottle and was enjoying talking to each other. That was till Mark had to ask about Jay.

Mark said "What do you know about what happened to Jay? Did you kill him?" He looked at me after asking with a mixture of anger and sadness in his face. I was not sure if he would start screaming at me, attack me, or break down in tears. Neither happened though and I did not keep him waiting long for me to answer him. I did not tell him what really happened or any details of what happened. I did say "Mark, I am sorry that you are in pain as we once were friends. I didn't feel bad about what happened to your brother. Jay had tried to have his guys kill me and he came after me himself while I was with Rose. If Jay was not already dead, I would put a bullet in his heart. He was a bad guy and bad for both of us. But you should know that Jay did not die by my hands."

We sat quietly on his porch for a while as the sun had set and a little light remained. I knew that I have stayed longer than I should of. I decided to leave and go home. When I stood up to walk away, I told Mark that I would give him two weeks that he would not have to worry about me. My guys will continue what they are doing to his guys, but no one would bother him. Then I walked off and got in my truck, and drove down the road. The moon did not give up any light and it was well hidden behind the clouds. The only light I was able to get was from the headlights of my truck.

The drive home was a sad drive. I expected my visit to give me a better insight into what Mark was thinking and if I had anything to worry about. Instead, I was reminded that once Mark and I were friends. We were not friends like I was with Duke, but for a time, we would hang out and talk. There were lots of times that I spent talking with Mark about where we plan to go and what we planned to do. It is funny to think that both of us wanted to get out of Ohio and do important things. I believed Mark once told me he wanted to be a firefighter, he even hinted at it that night. The thought of saving people, buildings, and a community excited him. If I remember correctly, I told him that I wanted to be an Architect. I always liked creating.

Instead of me creating, or Mark saving people; we both destroyed people and their hopes. I have always told myself that I only provided the people the option to do whatever they wanted to do. It was their choice to do what they want to do to themselves. I was only making money by offering them a choice. It is a debate that I had with myself several times after that. When my mind cleared, I came to realize that I still did not know what to expect from Mark. So I refused to think any more about the evening with Mark and how I enjoyed it.

Not long after that, I was back home. When I pulled in, I saw Rose's car parked by the steps. I parked next to her car and sat in my truck a few seconds after, I wanted to make sure my mind was clear. Rose did not need to know that my thoughts were weighing heavily on my mind. I lit a cigarette and looked up to see the front door open. Rose was standing there yelling down to me. I think she said my name, so I got out of my truck and told her that I am coming. There was no waiting anymore, so I walked up the stairs and gave her a big kiss while holding her close to me.

What a good feeling having Rose in my arms, was all I could think about. I felt all my muscles relax and felt as if I had not rested for a month. My arms let go of her and I melted down to one of the chairs next to my door. Rose sat in the chair that was on the other side of the door and asked what I have been up too. Since I promised to not keep any secrets from her, I told her.

I started with telling her about how excited Mick was when I told him I am letting him take on more and making him my partner. When I told her about him giving me a big bear hug, she started laughing as I did. Rose knew Mick and how he tended to be. We joked about it and how she is looking forward to the next time she sees Mick. I told her that the rest of my day was just general business things. She did not seem to care about any of that. I said that I went to Mark's house and sat with him for a few drinks. She gave me a look that made the summer sticky night air feel as cold as an Ohio New Year's day.

She angrily asked how I could sit with any Himlee after what they have done. The more she talked, the more I started seeing tears coming, till she busted out crying. She cried so much that you could have filled a bucket with her tears. I worked to calm her down and get her to stop crying. It was not an easy task since she felt so much anger and fear from what Jay Himlee did. Rose did not realize that Jay did everything on his own, as far as I knew. I understood that all she could think about what has recently happened. She remembered the guys following her and Jenny, the guys shooting at me, and the night Jay came to our hangout spot to threaten me personally.

Before I got a chance to tell her why I was with Mark Himlee, she asked if I was going to take care of Mark as I took care of Jay. This shocked me, but before she said anything more, I led her to sit in my truck with me.

I had a simple fear that there was possibly listening devices in my place. Let's say that I watched a lot of spy movies back then. My thought was that if someone overheard me talk about drugs, I would be able to explain it as general talk. But talking about a murder would have had me behind bars for life.

We both grabbed a smoke and took a few hits before we started talking again. I started talking and explained why we were in my truck. It took her a moment to understand my thinking about listening devices, but she agreed to humor me. Then I told her about how I saw Jay and grabbed him. From there I told her everything, but I did not get into details when I got to what we had Jay do. Rose did not need to know that that and I worried that she would have been scared of me or think I was a monster. Luckily the news left out a lot of details or the police did not tell the news all the details. Either way, I did not have to explain any of it to Rose and she did not ask.

Rose asked a few general questions about Jay, then asked why I was hanging out with Mark. This was an easier question to answer now that she was calm. I explained that I went to see if Mark was thinking that I killed Jay. I added that I took a bottle of bourbon to help ease tensions. We were in the middle of trying to put one another out of business by any means possible, as we were competitors. Rose had a blank look on her face and asked why I even cared.

I remember saying "If Mark thinks I killed Jay, he might let his anger or sorrow get the best of him and come after me. I wanted to understand where he was. If he would have tried to attack me, I would have killed Mark and anyone in his house. I like Mark and I would prefer to have him ran out of town. When I sat with him, he did not seem to blame me. He blamed Jay for his drug use and his anger getting the best of him. Mark did ask if I had anything to do with what happened to Jay. I told him the truth when I said my hands had nothing to do with what happened." I also told her how we sat talking about a bunch of other things and almost talked like old friends. It is still a nice memory to think back on.

I was not going to tell Rose that I enjoyed most of my time talking with Mark. I also did not want to think about doing it again. The fact is I might have to kill Mark, or he might kill me. It was hard to say what would of happen. I just know that I couldn't let my feelings get the best of me. If Mark and I are eye to eye with guns in our hands, I could be dead if I delay. I spend a lot of time alone while I was driving, and you never know when someone will catch up to you.

Rose and I finished talking about both the Himlee Issues and went into the house. We were ready to enjoy being together and let everything else drift away. It made me happy to be able to tell Rose all of this and I promised to tell her what is going on. I was not able to worry about hiding things from her and keep my mind on what I had to.

We also made two agreements when I promised to tell her the truth. The first one was the most important one. She agreed that she would not let anyone know that she knows anything that I did. She kept telling people that I was some kind of broker. This one kept her out the conflict and made sure she was safe per the agreement Mark and I made.

The other agreement Rose and I made is that we spend most of our nights not talking about my business. At least we did not bring it back up if we did not need to. It allowed us to have some real time together.

That is what we did, and we enjoyed our time for the rest of the night. The night was not long enough, but it was good to have Rose with me. No matter how long the night was, it was still good. We went inside my place and just sat on the couch together listening to the radio. I got back to feeling relaxed, I was content to be able to relax as long as I could. I knew I could let my guard down with Rose there.

Per the agreement that Mark and I made, if anyone breaks

our agreement, their entire family will be a target for punishment. The worst part is, the punishment could be anything. The person who had their family or friend attacked would be the one who could choose how to punish the people. This is why no one with half a brain would attack Rose or my family. No one wanted to have my personal attention and punishment.

Chapter Ten

It has been about a few weeks and none of Mark's guys or Mark himself has done anything towards my guys or me. I heard that Mark was trying to figure out who was going to be his new right-hand man, and he also had to deal with the guys who followed Jay. Those guys started to become independent sellers or would start working with Mick and me.

The downside of dealing in this type of work, people are only loyal if they think you can benefit them. With the Himlee brothers, some of the guys thought Jay would protect them. Jay told them he would stand up for them if someone attacked them or tried to take their territory, while some are with Mark to get better prices and police protection in their areas. Mark and I both knew who to pay off to keep things running smoother.

I know that I would have lost a large handful of guys if Mick left or died when he got stabbed. This is also why I made Mick my partner. Now that Mick was willing to kill, he would build a stronger reputation. This would give him the power to enforce anything he needed to. Most people listened to him out of respect or because they were afraid of what I would do. Since the fighting with the Himlees started, there has been a new set of rumors about me going around. There was even one that claimed that I killed Jay while making the police watch. It made me laugh to think that people believed I was that powerful.

There was another rumor that I had a hand in. It went that Mick and I were attacked by four of Himlee's guys. Then we shot them, but they were alive and we buried them alive to die from either bleeding or lack of air. Duke had told me that he heard this one a few times. What I always found odd about these rumors. No one asked about who the people were or if there was anyone missing. Instead, people never question a rumor that they wanted to believe. I knew this and that is why I put it out there. I figured that Mick has a bit harder attitude since we took out Jay. People would believe it more and it would work in his favor.

What I really liked about this quiet time between Mark and me was that I had time to focus on Mick. I was able to teach Mick a lot of things that he did not know that I did. Duke was also was able to show him what went into making the counterfeit money. Mick suggested that Duke took on an apprentice and I left that up to Duke to decide. From what I heard later, Mick and Duke discussed who to get when I was not around. That is when Duke decided that he would get out like I was. He wanted away from that life since I was getting out.

The things I did not teach Mick, he could pick up on his own. The only thing I left out of the information I gave Mick, was all my contact information. The fact is, knowing how to do something does not allow you to do it. The other important things that are needed is the money and knowing who to deal with. This did not go past Mick without him noticing. He even asked me why I did not give him John's information. I told him that it is simple security for me. I made him my partner and it is unlikely I would need to worry about him. I did not have to do this but felt it was right. On the flip side, if he got tired of being my partner and wanted to take over everything, what was going to stop him? Mick laughed and said nice point.

By the time I heard Mark was back running to his best ability, it was about a month after Jay's death. In that time, I was able to grow a bit more to where we were operating in Toledo, Lima, and a few more small towns. Mick and I both had to take on new seconds to manage the new areas. I had to focus a lot on Toledo though. I did not realize how many gangs were trying to sell drugs there, but they were small time. This made it easy when I went to a group in Detroit and made an agreement with them. I honestly did not know what all the group in Detroit did. I did know that they were not above being hired for some "relation" work.

It was a simple agreement. I would give them one percent of my profits from the area they handled. They would talk to anyone that was not covered by me or buying their supplies from me. With this agreement, it led to more than half the gang working with or for me. Each gang got an area to do their business and none of my guys would go there to sell. It was a simple agreement, but it was very effective.

Shortly after I settled my agreement with the guys in Detroit, I had to deal with a local guy. One of Mark's guys attacked one of my guys while he was making a deal with some people in a small town called Bradner, Ohio. I could only take this as either Mark was trying to take more territories from me or his guys did not fear me. Before I let this get out of hand, I called Mark and set up a meeting. This time, we were meeting out in the middle of the country. I warned Mark that I would bring Mick with me and will have guys sitting down the road. He agreed and said he will do similar. I gave him three days for us to meet and that gave me time to get things in order with Mick.

I found out through Mick, that a person can change fairly quickly. He had taken on a tougher image and I believed that it came from him killing Jay with his own hands. Mick did it out of the rage he had from Jay sending that girl and getting stabbed. Mick did not let things go. I have seen him hold a grudge for over a year before he got the guy alone and beat the guy up. I believed that guy only flirted with a girl he was seeing at the time.

It took me a while to talk to Mick. I paged him, but I knew he was running around distributing and collecting. So when he called me back three hours later, I explained what was going on and he needed to be a part of this now. I also asked if he could find someone that is a good long shot. With us being out around lots of little farm towns and farms, there was surely a few of the guys that go deer hunting.

Mick told me in a snarky tone that he had a guy or two that he will have come along. I told him before we hung up the phone that the guys don't need to shoot to kill, only wound or really scare them. With that being said, Mick made some kind of noise and said he will take care of his end of things. Then the phone went dead.

I decided to go to Bradner before calling it a day. I needed to hear from my guy what happened. I did not want to go and start the fighting upon hearsay. So when I got in town, I saw some kids that looked like potheads and asked if they knew where my guy was. I used his name at the time, but now I can't remember it.

The stoners were happy to tell me where to find him and that his higher prices are worth it, "if you know what I mean". Then they started to giggle. I had to believe that they must have smoked some before I ran into them. But they gave great directions and I was talking to my guy a few minutes after.

This guy had greasy hair, was small and young and not the best looking clothes. I knew of his family and selling drugs in this small farm town would be the best thing he would do. I remember his voice most of all. He had this deep voice, but he was a skinny freshman in high school. I would almost bet that if I backhanded him, he would not get up for a while.

When he first started to tell me what happened, he was getting excited as if he was going to tell about an epic battle. He did not even stop to think about what he was going to say, so I knew he had told his story many times. I stopped him after a minute into his story. I put it simply that I don't want the hype or anything other than the facts.

The guy calmed down and with a deep breath, started over. This time he told it as he remembered it before he hyped it up. He was about to drift off to his epic story, and you could hear it in his voice. Luckily he got back to the basics with a simple clearing of my throat. He said that it was no more than two young guys yelling at each other and pushed one another for a few minutes. The closest to a real fight these guys got into was my guy made a fist as he said, "The fire of hell almost came down". That is when I could no longer keep composed and I started laughing with that last statement.

The poor guy looked embarrassed and I felt bad for him. I imagine this was the most excitement he had as long as he could remember. The worst part of it, in my opinion, was that he was starting to believe the epic version of the story. If I waited to talk to this guy, he might have only remembered a bit of the real event. I have seen this from people a handful of times. Some don't have much to tell people about their own life, so they make a small event into a big deal.

Normally I didn't care when someone did this. I found it entertaining. Though this time it had spread to rumors going around. These rumors are making it sound like the fighting between Mark and I was back on. If I had to deal with fighting Mark, my plate would have been more than full. Between dealing with the Toledo Gangs and trying to build up my business in Lima, Mark would have run my full plate over.

I still feel odd about Mark and me fighting, considering how we started. When Jay got involved, it was not a surprise we started fighting. Since Jay has died, things were getting back to a smooth process. I did not know how Mark was doing, but my guys were making money. They were doing this since they were not fighting or watching out for some dumb ass to do something stupid.

I spent the remaining time before my meeting with Mark putting some personal issues in order. I did not want to have Mark catch me off guard and end me. I relocated my personal funds, contact book, and letters I had written to everyone close to me. Once I got everything in place, I called Duke. I told him where he could find everything plus the instructions for about $200,000 in cash. Duke sounded confused since he did not know about my meeting with Mark, but he agreed. All I had left to do was wait for Mick.

It seemed as I hung up the phone and Mick was at my place to have me ride with him for our meeting with Mark. As Mick and I went down the road, I started to tell him a thought I had about why Mark agreed to meet in the country. I don't know if it was my mind playing out the worst case scenarios, but I told Mick that Mark could be planning to shoot us. He could have planned to meet in the country because he doesn't want any other people getting hurt. I chuckled saying that he is being a nice guy if he only wants to kill us.

Mick smiled at me and said that we are covered, so there is nothing to worry about. He said two guys are hunting in the woods across the road and watching us. We also have four other guys waiting on the side of the road for us to show up. When I asked him how he got these guys to do all this, he said he promised some weed for the four guys to split. The same deal for the guys hunting and an ounce of weed if they have to shoot someone. Mick mentioned that they will not get anything if something happens and they don't come to help us. He reminded me that I suggested where we were meeting.

After all was said, we talked for a short time about football. We argued about that seasons Ohio State and Michigan game and made fun of our Browns. Mick loved his Buckeyes and was very vocal about it. I was a Michigan fan, but only got loud about it when I would be drinking and the topic came up. Now some of our football discussions get heated. This time, I thought Mick wanted to punch me, but we arrived and Mick pulled next to our guys. We sat for a few minutes to let Mick ask them if they are OK with the deal. They all said yes and we drove a quarter mile up the road.

When we got there, it was probably ten minutes later that Mark and his guys showed up. They came up the same way we did and his car of guys parked next to our guys while Mark parked in front of Mick's car. I personally would not do this, because he had to turn his back to us to get to his car. But I could have been over thinking things again. I was hoping that this would be nothing more than us talking and putting things to bed.

After few more minutes of sitting in their car, Mark got out and came back to us. The guy with him stayed in the car standing by the passenger side door. It was a nice day, so we all had our windows down and I would have bet that Mark's guy had a gun on the seat in his reach. We all had no trust in each other at that moment.

It didn't take Mark any time when he was walking to us. He

started talking. Mark started with acting like he was angry as he raised his voice but was not yelling. He did not say anything that mattered while walking to us. But when he reached Mick and me, we were sitting on the hood of Mick's care. Mark stopped in front of me and said "Well?"

It was interesting because I could swear that Mark was doing all this for his guys. As far as I was concerned, my guys knew when I really got upset to the point of showing it. So, I did not get up to play the same part Mark was playing. Instead, I calmly said, "Mark, you know Mick. He is now my partner and I want him to know everything I know. So, what I am about to say is not a shock to him. But do you know that both our guys in Bradner are full of shit? They are also fighting like little schoolgirls." Mark just looked at me without saying anything until I asked if he talked to his guy or just was going off the rumor. He said he did not know who his guy was, so he did not know who to talk to. I was not surprised as Mark was lazy in the sense that he did not go looking for information. He expected it and accepted what he heard.

I told Mark what my guy said with every sad little detail. Mark and Mick started to laugh when I added that the guy said he was going to bring down hell's fury. Mick caught himself laughing and stopped, but Mark kept going. With the tension broken, I went to the back seat of Mick's car and grabbed some folding lawn chairs.

Then we got to business and agreed that we would no longer fight with each other. It just is not profitable or beneficial for either of us. The three of us agreed to figure out territories and put a few simple rules in place. I figure it would take time to work out all the details.

With things in order, I invited Mark and his guys to come to the house for a little party. After Mark agreed, Mick said we can call it our peace party. Mark and I smiled and went back to our cars and on our own way.

The rest of the day was a good one. I rode along with Mick while he did some collections and invited about ten people to our peace party. It had been a good few months since I did any collections and some of the people we met up with were happy to see me. They wanted to talk and catch up, but I told them that we could do this at the party. Most of these guys were working under me when I was working for the other guy. I liked that guy. Now they have people selling for them and I guess you could call them Area Managers.

Once Mick got what he had planned to get done for the day, we head back to my place. We were about two miles away, and I invited him to join me for a gun deal with the group out of Detroit on the next day. I found another business opportunity that we both could benefit from. This deal would also allow me to introduce Mick to them and I knew Mick would have wanted to meet them. When we got to my place, Mick pulled out a black date book and said "that is Friday, I can do Friday. I will just be late for the party on Saturday."

Having never seen Mick keep a date book, I chuckled and said that is OK, we can wait for you. Without noticing my reaction to his date book, he just looked down at his book and did not pay any attention to me. After he finished making his notes, he looked up at me and said: "Kiss my Ass, I will see you tomorrow." I smiled and nodded, then started getting out of his car. Before I closed his door, a thought came to me as I realized his datebook is as valuable as my contact book. If someone gets a hold of Mick's date book, they could see what he does. This could be used by the cops as evidence to lock us up or by someone who wants to take our business.

I sat back down in his car and Mick gave me a look that meant to get out of my car. Before Mick got a chance to verbally tell me what his look was saying, I started talking again. "Mick, you know that my address book has everyone I deal with in it. If it got in the wrong hands, lots of people could end up in Jail or worst?" Mick just nodded telling me he understood what I said, so I continued talking. "You do realize that your little black book there has the same issue as my book?" I waited for real words from him, so I lit up a cigarette while waiting. Since he did not respond, I started to make a come on motion with my hand. That got him to respond, but Mick did not respond the way I figured he would.

He got defensive with me and I could only think that he took it that I was talking down to him. Mick said "Who do you think I am? Do you think that I don't know what I am doing?... I know this can get me in trouble and that is why you are the only one who has seen it." While Mick was huffing from being so worked up, I handed him one of my cigarettes and my lighter. When he started lighting up the cigarette, I started talking again. "Mick, I am not saying you don't know what you are doing. I am thinking that this could be used against me and a lot of people we deal with. I prefer to keep things going good. With Jay no longer an issue, we are expanding and Mark is coming to discuss terms so we both can work to grow. That is all I am thinking. I want you to protect that book as I do mine." As I took a breath, Mick said, "I will protect it, I agree with you. I did not think about it affecting anyone else. If we are good, I will pick you up tomorrow." I nodded and got out.

Mick drove off to somewhere I don't know. I knew Mick did not want to mess things up or be the reason that someone gets hurt. I did expect that Mick would mess up and let others know about his book down the road. I just hoped that Mick does not do something that makes me regret what I might have to do. This made me think about how Riggs and Dan had started this short little war that we had with the Himlee's. Dan wanted to be a big dog and Riggs did not want to let Dan go alone to a meeting I said was bad. Then Jay thinking he was big enough to take me on and used Dan and Riggs to start something. Now that Riggs stopped coming around, Dan is keeping his distance from me, and Jay is dead.

As all this ran through my head I walked up the stairs and back into my place. It has been a tiring time and I was starting to believe that I would get back to a mostly peaceful life. Not considering the few dealings I would have with people who would not pay or got behind, it would be nice. I even started to get excited thinking that I could start creating a real business structure. I thought how nice it would be to have things run smoother. I was smiling as I went through my door and telling myself that it all might have been worth the stress. With that, my door closed behind me and I did not worry about anything for the rest of the night.

Chapter Eleven

Another day and another sale. That is what I said to myself as I was getting my coffee. That was a good day for me as I was about to sell off a lot of firepower that I got from the guy who picked up Ferris. I did not realize that John was transporting that much at one time. I guess Mick gave the guy a hundred dollars to go to the house so he could unload the pickup truck the guy was driving. When I saw all that we got with the money, I was not sure I got a deal. After some research and a few phone calls, I learned how wrong I was. If I had to guess, these were from a Military Armory. I can say from personal experience that the P90 was very fun to shoot.

While I got around, I heard Mick come in and put down a set of keys slide on my kitchen island. I walked out with a towel wrapped around my waist to see Mick making coffee again. I jokingly asked if he needs anything, and without looking at me, he only said: "I could use some more rope." With that comment, I was confused about what he needed a rope for. I think he could tell he confused me, too. Mick followed up with saying that he used my spare set of keys to take my truck to load all the guns in it. I liked it when he said, "I put something to cover the guns between the tarp and the crates. Hope they don't mind a little mulch with their guns. If they bitch, you can say it's a bonus gift of goodwill." I only laughed and went back to my room to get around.

It was about five minutes when I came back out with an unopened reel of rope in hand. To my surprise, Mick had a cup of coffee waiting for me and my to-go mug sitting next to my cup. I did not ask why he had done this, but I sat down and put the rope on the countertop. Mick had a puzzled look on his face while staring at the rope. He made a few odd sounds that I guess was him trying to say something. Then with a cocky smile, he asked why I kept the rope in my bedroom. Since I was in a good mood and knew that we were about to make a lot of money, I joked and said, where do you keep that kind of stuff, you weirdo. With a shaking of his head, we got up and took our coffees to go.

After we tied the tarp over the guns and mulch better, we got on the road. We only had about an hour and a half drive to the Ohio and Michigan border. When we got outside of Toledo, there was an abandoned warehouse on the Michigan side. There was homeless that stayed in there and the cops don't bother them, so I wasn't concerned about one of them walking into our deal.

Everyone avoided the warehouse because of them and I guessed that no one cared as long as they did not burn the place down.

I let Mick drive up to the meet so I could think and play with the radio. It was a beautiful morning with a nice breeze. I even asked Mick if he would like to go golfing after the meeting. I was in the mood to play 9 holes and enjoy a nice sunny day. Mick did not reply to me: he just focused on the road ahead of him. I tried to make a few other comments about random things, but I still got nothing from him. So out of being annoyed by being ignored, I gave him a shove and he snapped out of whatever had him in a daze.

Mick had a concerned look on his face. When he looked at me, all I could say was "What?" I never believed people saying that they felt like something bad was going to happen before anything happened. I guess that is why I blew off Mick's concern when he said that he felt like this deal was a mistake. He even asked if we could cancel the deal and sell it off to someone else. He would have turned us around in the middle of the road if I would have agreed, but we were ten miles away. I shook my head to say no and Mick said OK. We drove the final ten miles in silence.

When we were just about to pull into the drive for the warehouse, and Mick stopped my truck and handed me my gun from the center console. He said that he has one on him already and he wants me to have mine with me or he would turn around. It took me a moment to realize how good of an idea to have my own gun was. These guys were part of some group in the Middle East who I found out later that called themselves freedom fighters. I did not understand at that time why someone saying they are a freedom fighter in their country but came to here. We now would call them a terrorist.

I put the gun in its holster and clipped it to the inside of the back of my pants. Now that Mick had me thinking about this and it was only the two of us, I got in my glove box and grabbed my little six shooter. It was small enough that I could put on my ankle without anyone noticing.

Mick laughed and started driving down the drive towards this old warehouse. I first noticed some of the doors had fallen off the tracks and the green paint was faded. I could easily tell that the owner gave up on trying to sell the property. The grass seemed to have been as tall as my waist and the bushes were so overgrown that they were coming over into the drive. It was clear to see why the druggies that do crack and heroin would come there. Most of them became homeless after selling everything they had to get more drugs. When they have nowhere to go, they stayed in the warehouse.

As we drove along the side of the building I saw our not overly friendly customers inside in one of the openings. They were standing next to an old caddy trying to look tough. They mostly were dressed in tees and jeans, but the main guy was tall with grey hair, beard, and had on some kind of tan suit. You did not see people dressed like that back then. I don't know what it was about that suit, but it was not like any other suit I have seen before.

The guys in the blue jeans looked as they was nervous or planning something. I only figured that by how they would rock on their feet and fiddle with their hands. Don't think they looked timid or scared, they looked as if they were trying to look tough. I almost laughed when I saw a short stocky guy was puffing out his chest but had to relax and slouch.

After my contact in the tan suit stepped forward, I got out of the truck and walked into the building. Mick sat in the truck with the door open. He was waiting for a signal to come in. I had an agreement with Mick that if anything happens to me, use one of the P90 or CR–21 guns that we had in the truck. The nice thing about selling guns, you tend to have demos ready to show. This is why under my favorite soft blue blanket in the back seat, we had demos loaded and ready to show off. As I told Mick when we planned to do this deal, I don't want to die, but if I do make sure they all do too.

With that in my mind, I walked up to the guy in the tan suit and he said that Maj something had sent him to deal with me. He also said his name and I don't remember it or care what it was, I just remember his tan suit. I started getting the same feeling that Mick had. I don't think the guys there remembered Mick was just out at the truck with all the guns. The only reason I say this is because two of them started to move to my sides and almost behind me. I was very happy Mick did not wait to see what was going to happen. When the guys got out of my line of sight, I heard Mick yell Bearman. Without a thought, I turned to see the guys with knives pulled out. They looked as they were going to attack me. Like I told Mick, I don't want to die. So, I did not wait for them to act and I pulled my gun. I don't know if it was Mick or me that shot first. We did not stop till no one with a weapon was standing.

When Mick and I were done, only two guys were left. I did not get as lucky as I have in the past. One guy stabbed me in the right shoulder. I could not believe that I got stabbed, but I knew that someday it would happen or I would get shot. I used to joke that I am shocked by how I have not been hurt any more than a broken bone here and there. Now, this guy mistakenly put his cheap not- made in the USA knife in my back. The damn knife's handle wobbled and broke when I turned around. The guy looked me in the eye with a shit eating grin. That was, till I put my last bullet in the guy's balls. He was screaming and what I take as cursing in whatever language he spoke. Considering he laid there for another half an hour after everything, I did not expect him to do well. When his friends picked him up, they took him off to what looked like a box truck back in the shadows of the warehouse.

But once the fighting was done, Mick got the knife out of my back. I was not thrilled when Mick poured my Makers Mark out of my flask and on my back. He then took the first aid kit from my toolbox and bandaged me up. Mick told me to wrap my shoulder with my shirt. He said it would help stop the bleeding. While was getting me taken care of, the guy in the tan suit walked towards us. He walked with his hands up to show that he did not intend to do anything. So I talked with him and the CR-21 next to me. I found out the guy that was dragged off to a box truck and the other guys had recently come in the country together. They was sent to help the cause. His boss warned him that they seemed to want to make a name for themselves, but he did not know how. The three of us talked for a while and made an agreement for the guns with an extra ten percent on top of the forty-two thousand dollars. Plus Mick and I kept one of each gun for our own toys. Mick would not give up that CR-21 after everything that had just happened.

Once we shook his hand and motioned to the other guy who remained by the car, the box truck in the shadows drove up. The driver of the box truck and the other guy unloaded my truck. My new friend Mr. Tan Suit handed Mick four bags of cash and gave me a couple of stacks of cash. I started to check the cash to make sure it was real. I had no need for forty-six thousand dollars of counterfeit. I could make that myself for about a thousand and not get stabbed. Not that you can't tell, but I am still bothered that I got stabbed.

Mick saw how I was checking the money, and he started doing it to the cash in the bags. After a few minutes, Mick nodded yes and a smile. I took it as he was telling me that it was all real. On that note, I said goodbye to those guys and got in my passenger seat and Mick got back behind the wheel. As Mick started the truck, Mr. Tan Suit came to the driver side window. He said, "If we do another deal, I will only bring people I trust. See, the guys I have don't bring knives to a gun fight. They also don't do anything unless I tell them."

I gave a quick response of, "as long as we don't stab each other in be back, I think we will be fine". We all shook our heads in agreement and Mick started driving. Now that I started to relax, the pain from the new hole in my shoulder came on full force. I started to get light headed and shortly before I blacked out, I heard Mick said, "Hold on, I have someone in Rossford...." and I know he said more, but I was out. The next thing I know, I woke up on a workbench in a garage. I noticed that the pain was not as bad and my shoulder was properly bandaged. Still, in a little daze, I rolled off the bench and fell to the concrete floor on my other shoulder. When I looked around, I saw Mick and some guy at the passenger side of my truck with what I thought was a vacuum.

Mick must have heard me fall or looked towards me because he came over and picked me up. I started to ask questions, but I am not sure if I was speaking clearly. Whatever pain medicine I was on had me loopy as hell. Mick helped to a lawn chair and handed me a cup of orange juice with a straw. After trying to focus, I started to understand what I was hearing. The first thing I heard was "This will get the blood out."

When I stood up and started to walk towards Mick and the guy, this mystery guy came over to me. He said, "Let's get you a shirt before everyone sees your bandages." He walked into his house and I followed him in. I only wanted to know what was going on and who this guy was.

It was a nice home and the table had been set up with gold trimmed plates. Since it was only a bit past noon, it had to be set up the night before. As I was looking around and getting more of a feel of the place, he walked into the dining room where I was snooping.

I had to guess he was a doctor because he walked in saying "Let me make this simple. You got stabbed and lost some blood. Luckily it was not enough that you needed a transfusion. So I cleaned you up and stitched you. I am giving you a clean tee shirt so you don't have something covered in blood. All you need to do is clean the stitches with rubbing alcohol for about two weeks and change the bandages. You should have nothing to worry about. After two weeks, just cut the stitches. You can pull them out from there."

Since he finished talking and looked at me with a blank stare, I asked if he was done. With a nod of his head, I started to ask questions. I only remember asking, who are you, where am I, and what he was getting out of this. I did not get to ask anything more when he started to answer me. He started with telling me that I can call him Max and we were at his house. As for what he got out of it, he said Mick paid him already. He told me to finish cleaning my truck and leave. After that, he walked me back to the garage where Mick was pushing the vacuum back into the garage.

I walked up to Mick and he said that he is ready, and the truck is clean. When I opened my mouth to say something, Mick stopped me before I said something. He said we would talk in the truck. I agreed because I was tired and I wanted to get home at that point, so I just climb into the passenger seat. To my surprise, a wet seat gave me a wet ass and back, which lead to the first question when Mick got into the truck. As I waited for Mick, I watched him be friendly with Max and gave him a quick hug like you give a family member. Mick got into the truck and started to drive us back to my place.

As soon as we got out of the driveway, I asked Mick why my ass is wet. He started to laugh and I was not in too much of a mood to be laughed at. He asked me if I saw him cleaning my seat. I said yes and that is when he said that he was using a steam cleaner and told me how it worked. I know it sounds stupid not to know what a steam cleaner was. Just remember that all the ones I had seen were connected to some guy's van with a long hose. After a few jokes from Mick at my expense, we moved on.

We had a forty-five-minute drive, which turned out to be more than enough time for Mick to explain how he knew Max. It turned out that Max and Mick's dad were friends at that time. While Mick was there with his dad before; a guy showed up that was hurt and did not want to go to the hospital. Max fixed up the guy and Mick's dad explained that Max ran two practices. One was where he was a family doctor that you would go to with your insurance and have a medical record. The other practice was for the people who don't want questions asked and pay in cash. I also learned that it cost me twelve hundred dollars to be fixed up and get a new shirt. I can't complain because nothing was reported or written down. This fortunately meant that I did not have to talk to a cop.

I was happy to have spent the money to get fixed up. I saw

Rose's car sitting at my place when we were a mile away, and I could only think how fired up she would get. I asked Mick if he wanted to come in, and he did not wait till I finished talking to say "Hell no". He explained why he did not want to come in. If I remember properly, I think he said something more along the line of he would rather go back to fighting the guys from Detroit. He knew how Rose would react to me getting stabbed. I understood what he was saying. I would have rather gone back to fight again than tell Rose. I made her a promise, so I had to face up to how ever she took it.

By the time Mick stop laughing, we parked next to his car. With a quick goodbye and me reminding Mick about the party the next day, he got in his car to leave. It did not take him long to get on his way.

I went into my place where Rose was doing some cleaning. She stopped cleaning and came to give me a big hug and kiss. When she wrapped her arms around me, she hit my new stitches and I winced.

Once I winced, Rose grabbed my arm and turned me around. She was as quick as a rabbit trying to get away. I say this because she had the back of my shirt up and looking at my bandages before it registered. I had to explain the whole day up to the point that I got home. She knew what I was doing that day, so I could talk in general terms and she did not ask questions.

Rose knew what was going on, but it did not stop her from freaking out about some people trying to kill me. I thought she had prepped herself while I was dealing with Jay Himlee trying to kill me.

I had to think that as a concept, it is easy to think about what would happen. It is easy to think you are able to deal with these things coming. But when something happens, you realize that it is not what you thought it would be like. Watching Rose's face while I explained everything, you would think she was in more pain than I was. It tore me apart to see her like this and knowing she felt helpless through it all. After a bit of me generalizing things, she asked for us to go for a drive. I knew that she wanted to hear everything in the full details. Rose knew that I would not get into too many details in my place. My feeling that someone might be listening to me was always in the front of my mind.

As we drove, I explained that I shot two guys and killed one while the other most likely died. If he did survive, he would not have sex again. Mick shot a few guys and we did what we had to do or we would not have come home. The more I was telling her everything openly, I could see that she was pulling away from me in what looked like fear. Rose was told that I was a bad boy before we met, but in a farm town kind of area, you don't have anyone doing more than fist fighting. She had heard stories of me beating up people and putting a few in the hospital. She thought a bad boy would bother her parents and she even told me that she figured we would of only last for a few months. She planned to go back to the good boys who studied hard and most likely would go to college.

While we drove around, I made some stops and did a little business. It gave her time to think about what I said and we could keep working forward. That was at least what I was thinking. I explained while we drove around that I had my party with Mark Himlee the next night. It was to let everyone see that we are no longer fighting and are working together. Then she stopped me in mid-sentence. "Was Jay's suicide you're doing? Did you kill him too?" She took a breath and finished with "You said you did not put a hand on him, but that does not mean you did not do it. What did you do? I deserve to know if we are going to get married. I want to know what kind of man I will spend my life with." I took it as a good sign that Rose was still wanting us to get married.

With some thinking, I told her what happened. I explained how I would have not done anything to him, but Jay sent guys after her. I needed to make sure no one thought they could do that. As I told Rose about why Mick and I took out Jay, she began to relax. She made a comment about it means a lot that I would protect her. She said she always figured I would do anything to protect her, but she never thought it would have to include killing someone. By the time she was starting to come back around, we were passing through Gibsonburg. There was a bakery at the corner of 300 and 600 that we used to enjoy going to for some flavored ice. I know, it was a small town, but it was simple and was great on a summer day.

I parked in front of the bakery and went in to get us some flavored ice. When I got back she suggested that we walk to the park a few blocks away. During our walk, I went to hold her hand and she pulled it away then put her hands in her back pockets. I can say that I was hurt by that and a bit scared that she might reconsider being with me. It was a heartbreaking thought at that time. I took it she could read what I was thinking on my face. Because she told me that she wasn't going anywhere, but she needed time to process everything.

We walked some more and Rose asked her questions. I could tell when she was about to ask about killing Jay or the fight at the deal earlier. Rose would get quiet and pull me close so she can speak in my ear. As serious as this was for her, it was like she trying to kiss my face. It surprised me when some of her questions were not about what had happened, but what will happen to us. She wanted to know if I was always going to do this kind of work. I told her that when she goes to college, I will give everything to Mick to deal with. I would come with her and get an honest job. She did not say anything more while we finished walking and drove home. Once we got back to my place, she said that she was going back to her mom's and will be back tomorrow. I reminded her that I would be home late, but I want to see her. With that said, Rose drove off and I went into my place for the night.

Chapter Twelve

I did not sleep well thinking about what Rose was going to do. I realized that she is taking on a lot in such a short time and now she learns that what I do can get me killed or seriously hurt. I don't expect her to accept what I do and what might happen. She is no longer in danger with Jay gone and if she left me, she would not have to worry about gangsters or thugs. I thought about how smart Rose was and if I can figure this out, so could she. The smart choice was for Rose to leave and become the woman that makes the world a better place. I was realizing I was the type who destroys and anything I build causes pain.

With all this still on my mind and being tired, I forced myself to push it all aside. I had to think about the party. After all, this party was to show that the fighting was over. It would not be easy for some to accept since there has been lots of tension between my guys and Mark's guys. Over the last year, they would fight and screw with each other. One of Mark's guys was trying to get my guys business. He told people that my guy was putting his pubic hair and oregano in the weed he sold. As a way to get even, my guy starts sleeping with his sister to make him even angrier.

So I had to do what I could do to make sure that things did not start up again. Before I realized it was morning. I ran out of the door once I had my coffee and keys. My first stop was the drive-thru in Gibsonburg. I had to buy a keg of beer, cheap whiskey, and some Makers Mark for Mark and me to split. This was the easiest part of my day. Once everything was in my truck, I was off to the house.

When I got there, I saw Duke parked by an old small barn that sat back on the property. After I put everything away, I walked back to find the cellar door open. I yelled down to let Duke know I was coming down. I put a shotgun down there because that is where Duke made the counterfeit money. If someone came down uninvited, they would know very quickly they are not to be down there. As I walked down the steps, I heard Duke call out, "Who is there? I have a loaded twelve gauge." I started to laugh and yelled back to Duke saying "Remember to use the trigger to shoot as I showed you." I did not hear anything until I walked into the cellar front room. I heard Duke call me an asshole while putting the gun down. That is when I knew it was safe and walked into the room that was added to the existing cellar.

This was a nice size room with concrete walls, floor, and

ceiling that we used to print the counterfeit money. I did not dig it or know why it was made, just figured that the previous owner was afraid of someone finding something. Either way, we worked in a hole in the wall and made plenty of money doing it. When I walked into the room, Duke was making us money. I had no idea why he was doing this. I never said anything to him about needing more.

Since there was no harm in him getting ahead of the demand, I took a seat on a gray bucket. We talked about all sorts of things and joked about our girls. The one thing that struck me while we were talking was Duke said he wanted to marry Jenny. He told me that it was on his mind ever since I got engaged to Rose.

I thought that was great news. Duke was with Jenny for a few years during high school and they were very close. With this news, I told Duke to get me fifty thousand dollars printed. With that money, I would try to get him twenty thousand in real money so he could buy a house. It only made sense to me that they had a nice home to start off in. Duke was smiling as big as I had ever seen, and I went back to the house.

To my surprise, Mick and three guys were standing outside the house looking it over. By the time I got up to them, I heard Mick saying he wants the roof fixed too. That is when I said "too?" And with it being Mick, he had to try and play it cool. With a half look over his shoulder, he said that he wanted to fix it up. I did not understand his need for this until I walked into the house. There in one of the bedrooms was Mick's stuff thrown in the corner.

I turned around to go outside so I could talk to Mick, but when I got into the middle of the front room, he walked into the house. Mick knew what I was going to say to him. He explained that Max told his dad about fixing me up. His dad freaked out, then before Mick got to explain, he was homeless within 30 minutes. That was when he took over my house.

We sat down and talked about what completely happened. I did not realize that Mick's dad was a cop and they had been fighting for over a year. Mick said that his mom left a few years back, but he still sees her once or twice a month and he smiled when talking about her. He told me how his dad slowly started drinking more and more. Mick said that his dad never got physically violent, but it got close. It sounded like it had been very tense with constant fighting. With everything said, I told Mick that I had no problem with him staying at the house. I don't want people walking around unsupervised with everything we do there. With a nod, I got up and said, do what you need to.

Now that I had everything in order with Mick, I had to go. I needed to meet with a few of my "Area Managers" who I wanted to make sure that they would be coming to the party. This had to be a smooth process and a good time for both sides. I did not want Mark to change his mind.

I knew that Mark never really wanted to fight. It did nothing good for either of us. I would not have told anyone other than Mick, but if Mark wanted to start fighting again, I would have to worry about him and those guys in Michigan. I worried that it would not end well for me. With no more reason to stay around, I was off to Fremont.

There was a guy named Kyle who was a friend of Mick's and worked under him. I did not care where he came from or how he got to running some guys in Fremont and the little areas around. Kyle did a good job at what he did. He had balanced the ability to be as feared as a junkyard dog and as friendly as any guy I had met. He very well could be good at taking my position, but he lacked the ability to be diplomatic. More times than I can count, I had to bail him out with the local Fremont police for being an asshole to them. It only took me talking with them for a few minutes and he was free again. I did not think they wanted to do the paperwork on him, so it was a way they used to remind him that he was not in charge.

I drove around Fremont for an hour till I found Kyle in the Walmart parking lot laying in the bed of his truck. Once I saw him, I pulled up next to him and got out. This guy did not even look at me as he thought I was a big boss. He might have been considered a boss in Fremont, but he knew who the big boss was. He showed that he remembered when I said: "Kyle, what the HELL are you doing?" Kyle sat up and Looked at me then said: "Bearman, what are you doing here?"

I sat on his tailgate and we talked a bit about how his business was going and the party. I told him that I wanted to make sure that he remembered about the party and to play nice with whoever Mark brings. Kyle told me that he and the other "Area Managers" met up the night before. I did not know they did this, but he explained that they found that it helps them a lot to meet up. Kyle said that he had to help Jason who is working in the Toledo area with some issues. I did not know there were any issues either. For another twenty minutes I listened to what they discussed and what they did without me knowing. I was very proud that they were working together as they were. I know Mark's guys were all for themselves and would rather cut you than help. The only problem with that was most of them was too scared to even pull a knife.

Knowing that all my "Area Managers" were set to come to the party, I decided that I had a chance to go back to my place. I could have used a short nap. It was a good thought at the time, and a shame it did not happen. That was because after I said my goodbye to Kyle and went to open my truck's door, someone came up behind me and grabbed my neck. Before I realized it, I was pushed against my truck. My first thought was that someone got me and my story was about to end. Instead, I heard my biological father Cameron starting to yell at me. All I could do was to twist around till I broke free. Once I was free, I saw Kyle was coming towards us and had a knife in hand. That was till I pushed my so-called father away and held up my hand to stop Kyle.

I heard Kyle ask if I was OK and I nodded my head, even though I most likely had a hand print on the back of my neck. I heard when Cameron started to tell me that I am embarrassing him and the rest of the Bearman family. I let him let talk because I knew Kyle was there and there was nothing too bad he could do to me. That is when Cameron Bearman surprised me. I opened my truck door to get my pack of smokes. When I reached in, I felt the door get slammed into my shoulder. I was in such pain with the door pressing on my knife wound. Kyle watched this and did not wait for any other reason to get up and put his knife against Cameron's side. With that warning, the door was no longer pinning me to my truck.

I was glad I am a lefty because it was my right shoulder that pinned against the truck. The reason I was happy for this fact was this was the first time I put a left hook on the side of Cameron's jaw. He only took a step back, but the look on his face said that he knew that I was no longer going to back down from him. In all truth, he could of kicked my ass, but that was no longer the point. I was not going to let him do it without a fight. That day was the last time I saw or heard from Cameron. He said while he was walking away from that I was not his son and he never wanted me to start with. That made me happy and affirmed what I already knew. Good riddance.

Kyle noticed that my shirt had some blood on the back of it. You probably could guess it was where I have been stabbed. The door must have put enough pressure to cause some blood to come out. I kept hearing Kyle asking me why am I bleeding and generally freaking out. While he was doing that, I pulled out my first aid kit and explained how I got stabbed and stitched up. Once I finished, I handed him a few things to clean and cover my wound.

While Kyle was wiping off the blood, he said that he never thought that it was true that I did everything he heard. He thought I was pushing drugs and girls. The fact of selling guns, blackmail, and other things he thought was not true until that day. I explained to him that it was easy to say I would not do this, then do that. Once you do that, this thing does not seem to be as bad. Next thing you know, almost nothing is off limits. He quickly finished bandaging me up. I turned to him and said "I do what is needed. It takes a lot to keep the cops and the competition down."

This time when I reached in for a cigarette out of my truck, I got it and enjoyed my smoke. I sat for another twenty minutes talking with Kyle to help him relax. We talked about what rumors were true and what was blown out of context. You could guess that a lot was blown out of context. It was funny to hear all the things he thought he knew about me. I remember one story he said that I started on my own by robbing a police station. From what he told me, I blackmailed a cop to help me and that was also how I got the police on my payroll.

I explained that Mark and I started together while we worked under a guy in Fostoria named Deatz. We were trusted by that guy till the day that he was found dead in a car accident. That is when I told Kyle about a conversation with John after a month of working for him. John told me it was funny that my previous boss died driving drunk. He also said that my boss always refused to drink, but loved to smoke his weed. Kyles' eyes got wider and he realized that I am not the real boss. Like him, I have someone above me that is scarier than I am. The difference between Kyle and me is that he knows that I have a boss. I don't know if John works for anyone or if he is the top of his ladder. I still remember when I realized that I am not really the boss.

It happened the day that I met John for the first time. In person, it was only three years ago, but it seems like a lifetime ago. He made it clear that I might be seen as the big man in this part of Ohio. He does not care who people think is the big guy in this part of the world. He only cares that I remember what happened to the guy before me who forgot his place. That was the first time I learned what true fear was. Ever since I talked to

John, I know that he lets me think I am getting a deal from him. I knew it is his choice what I get and what I would be paying. I did not think that Mick would handle knowing all the details about who was really in charge. This is me getting sidetracked again.

I finished talking with Kyle and went on my way home. After my drive home, I felt the world pulling me down, I walked in and went straight for my bed. I threw the comforter on the floor and flopped on the bed. Just as I was about to fall asleep or maybe I was in and out, I heard someone come in. I knew it had to be one of three people. It turned out to be Rose.

She did not say anything to me but laid down next to me and we wrapped our arms around each other. We laid there with a breeze coming in the window, lightly blowing on us. I fell asleep in no time after I stopped thinking about what she had to say. I came to the conclusion that she was there with me and she was willing to work through whatever we needed to. We both had to be tired because I just closed my eyes when Duke was shaking to wake me up. When I opened my eyes, there was Duke staring at me and Rose. She was sleeping looking as beautiful as she always did. I was happy that we were dressed when Duke came in. Sadly for Duke, it would not have been the first time he saw me naked. Considering I made a few bets over the time we had known each other where I would have to streak.

By the time I looked back to Duke, he was already at my door walking out of my bedroom waving me to get my ass up and moving. I figured that Duke was getting me up for the party, I did not know how he knew I was home. Kind of creepy to think he knew where I was, but when I got out to the living room, he told me that Kyle showed up to the house, then did not wait to tell the story of Cameron attacking me and how he stood up for me. What I remember Duke said was that it sounded like another epic story. He said that he has seen Cameron doing a lot worse than that and always doing things to be controlling. Duke to not sticking around to hear the rest of the story.

That is what lead him to my place and waking me up for the party. I am glad he did too. Most likely I would have slept for much longer and been late. Call me funny, but the host of a party should not be late. In my opinion, he should be the first one there. Not to be one to be late, I grabbed a bag of good weed that I kept under my sink so my mom would not see it when she came over and out the door we went. As we walked down the stairs, Duke said he was going to crash at my place and would ride with me.

I was OK with Duke riding with me since he normally would drink a lot. I would be happy to sip on my bourbon and smoke a joint. So we got on our way down the road when Duke just could not hold in his question anymore. Duke asked if I killed Jay and did I kill the guy who stabbed me. I know he had his theories, but most times Duke would go by the saying that, he can't answer anything he does not know. This was in regards to being questioned by a cop about my business. He liked it that way and it made him feel as if he was not doing anything wrong outside of printing some money. We would joke that he was just helping the government print money faster.

I don't know why he wanted to know this now, but I answered him by asking him about how much of the details he wanted. After he sat for a minute thinking about it, he said that he just wanted enough to know what rumors are and what is not. So I explained what happened with Jay. I told the story up till the point of Mick pulling up and finished that story with "by the time we left, Jay was no longer alive." Then I followed up with saying that the guy who stabbed me at the gun deal is most likely dead. I don't know for sure, but if he did, his death and the other guys that died are on my shoulders. I could not blame Mick or Jay or those guys up in Michigan. I set everything up and I made the choices to have those events happened. Anything Mick did was to protect me and himself."

Duke looked concerned and asked me to pull over so he could drive. I did not notice the tear coming down the side of my face. I listened to Duke because he has never asked me to do this before. There on country road 55 I pulled over and started to walk around the truck to trade seats with Duke. When I got to the tailgate, I could not help myself. I grabbed the bumper and sat on the ground crying. Up to that point, I never cried like that and I was not able to even talk.

I heard my truck turn off and then I saw Duke come to the back of the truck. When I saw him, I tried to pull myself together and get up. He helped me up and dropped the tailgate so I could sit on it. I don't remember how long I cried before I said anything.

When I did talk, I told Duke that none of this was supposed to happen. With a few sniffles getting in there, I continued to say that I was going to leave with Rose when she went to college. Rose and I planned to travel the United States the following summer. She wanted to see Niagara Falls and explore Yellowstone and so much more. Now I am ending one short war after killing a guy and worrying that I might have started something else. This time it is with some guys that I sold a ton of guns to.

Duke told me that there is nothing he can say to help, but we can stare at the stars. We sat there for a bit looking up at the sky until a car stopped to see if we needed help. Since I pulled myself together and I was back to myself, we thanked the guy and got back on the road. I also was the one behind the wheel and finished driving to the house.

I was glad to get all that out of my system. I felt a lot better, but I wished that Duke was not there. I was glad that if it had to be anyone there that it was Duke. I knew that he would never say anything about this to anyone. To also make it better, when we were a mile from the house, he lit up a joint and said that I need a reason for my red eyes. He was right, too. Showing up with a joint in hand, no one will question your eyes. That was the excuse we used to get a jump on the party. There was always a reason to smoke a joint back then.

When I pulled in, I saw that Mark was getting out of his car with two guys and another car had four guys get out. I only could assume that they were his guys. As I turned off my truck, Mark and his guys walked over to Duke and me. Duke handed me the joint and said, "Let's go."

If I saw these guys coming towards me just a week or two ago, I would be reaching for my gun, but that would cause more problems this time. I got out and reached out my hand to Mark. As his guys watched, I noticed Mick and a few of my guys on the porch watching too.

Mark took my hand and pulled me in for a friendly guy hug. It was as we used to do before we both went on our own. I took up with John in New York and Mark went with a guy in Chicago. We stopped being friends and had others pushing us to sell more and get rid of the competition. We both tried to run the other out of business by taking each other's customers. We never wanted any violence to occur. That was Jay who thought he had to do what he saw in the movies.

When I was chest to chest with Mark, he asked he we should tell our guys that this is a party and they need to relax. Then we let go of our embrace and I spoke loud enough that everyone could hear. "Let's drink and smoke, but for Christ sake loosen up." And with that our small party started.

Chapter Thirteen

I knew it would not be easy for everyone to get along at this party. I only hoped that they would. So we ended up going in to drink and smoke a little weed to enjoy the night. Once the twelve of us sat down on the porch and in the yard, we had a few drinks. It was not long till everyone started to laugh about the crazy stories that have happened. A lot of the stories were between customers and some cops trying to arrest them. I had to think they forgot that Mark and I were friends before all of this. It caught all the guys except for Duke when Mark and I told about our first deal together. Now when I say a deal, I mean something more than selling a dime bag.

After an hour or so of everyone hanging out together, the guys started to make bets on who could do some stupid shit. It was funny to watch, but Mark and I stayed on the porch while they ran off. I could hear Duke joking with one of Mark's guys. Then Mark pushed me on my shoulder and asked if I remembered our conversation at his place.

I let him know that I remembered everything we talked about. That is when he said "Bearman, I am leaving in about a month and I am not coming back. I have two options to get the money I think I will need." For a few minutes, we both sat in silence looking at each other.

"What the hell are you talking about? Where are you going and what are you going to do?" This is how I answered him. I guess I should have asked what options he was talking about. He would have not mentioned that unless it had something to do with me. The only reason I know I should have asked about the options was because of what he said. "Bearman, let's talk about my options first and you can listen to an offer I have for you. Now before you say anything, understand that you can either take my offer or I can turn my book over to another guy." I did not know there was another guy that could take and run Mark's guys and his supply line. While I was trying to figure out who could be the new person, Mark continued. He said "I could turn everything over to you. You would no longer have any competition in our area. This will make things peaceful." That got my attention and that would have been the best option for me.

Now I had to ask and see what it would cost me. Mark did not keep me waiting when he told me that he wanted fifteen grand in real cash and five grand in counterfeit money. I made him a counteroffer of twenty thousand in real cash and no counterfeit.

That was a deal I could do and Mick would not fight me over this deal. We agreed and shook hands. With that, I said: "Now that we are done with that, tell me what is going on." He told me everything. Come to find out, Mark had been thinking about our discussion. The one when we talked about what we really wanted to do instead of pushing drugs. He said that he would be going to out to Wyoming to fight fires and do rescues at Yellowstone National Park.

After we talked, he started making calls. He got himself into a training program where they will have him working at Yellowstone. It started in two months from the night of the party and he wanted to leave Ohio in a few weeks. Mark wanted time to settle into his new life. Mark told me about what would be involved for him to get through the training. It sounded like a lot and would take hard work to make it. We talked about this for about another ten minutes. The only reason we stopped was because Mark saw some of the guys coming back towards us. Before they did reach us Mark asked me to keep it to myself. I somewhat agreed and told him I had to tell Mick about our deal. Mark told me that he understood and agreed.

The party went on for about two more hours until he and his guys decided it was time to go. I thought it had to be about ten o'clock at night. My guys left about thirty minutes later. That left Duke, Mick, and me sitting on the porch to have one more drink before Duke and I would go on our way. It seemed like Duke was buzzed since his eyes were a bit glassy and he kept running his hands through his hair. I told them about the deal that Mark and I made. Mick jumped up yelling "Are you serious? We have no more competition?" He drank his glass of my bourbon like it was a shot and then poured himself a strong helping of bourbon. You could easily see how happy Mick was.

This made me sad. I could not stop thinking that I am losing a friend that I just got back. I could not blame Mark, I was planning on leaving in a year too. I guess the bourbon was getting to me, so I told Duke that we should go. Duke did not say anything but just crawled into my trucks back seat. I told Mick that I will have Duke put together the money in a week and I will set up a meeting for the three of us. I turned to get in my truck and drive home. As I started to climb into my truck, I yelled back to Mick and said: "You better not drink all my bourbon or you better replace it."

Mick waved his hand in the air when I was pulling out to get home. The stars were out and I don't think there was a single cloud in the sky. If I did not have to get on the main road, I could have easily driven home with no headlights. The moon seemed that bright and I was thinking that this could be a sign to how the rest of my future would be. After some thought about Mark leaving, I realized that I will miss him since we had gotten past everything. I was hoping that we could work together and to have a three-way partnership. We could have grown much larger than what I already did. I accepted that Mark was going and getting out would be best for him. Not many people like us get away with doing what we do forever, it catches up to you. That is also why I was looking forward to the following summer. Rose and I would be getting out of Ohio too. I was planning on starting a legal business. With how things finished that day, it got me thinking of telling Mick my plan to turn everything over to him.

By the time I pulled into my place, Duke was waking back up. He slept from the time he got into my truck. Once I got the truck parking brake set, Duke was already out of the truck and almost in my place. I did not wait a moment in my truck this time. I wanted to get back inside and tell Rose about everything. I even told her about Mark leaving to go fight fire fires and rescue people. She talked about how great that sounded. Duke said Mark always seemed to want to be a hero. Rose said that she did not realize he was that kind of person. I found it curious to see the difference between Rose's and Duke's response.

Duke knew Mark as long as I had. It was back when I was dating a girl named Sara. That time was only about having fun, making a little money, and not caring about what was going to happen. Rose had never talked to Mark, but she heard about him and his brother. Then she had to deal with the day that Jay had some of his guys put fear into her. I know Jay was trying to make me scared by doing that. So Rose was now hearing stories that Duke and I had about things Mark used to do with us. She was seeing a whole other side of Mark. We talked about how things turned out and what happened in the friendlier days. There was some joking about random things till about one in the morning. Duke crashed on my couch while Rose and I went into my bedroom.

We slept in till about nine in the morning. That was, till I heard a knock on the door. When I walked out to the living room, I noticed that Duke was already gone. I also noticed my stepdad Paul standing at my door. I had forgotten to call him and cancel our Sunday round of golf. Paul was upset that I was not ready to go or did not have a pot of coffee ready. After telling him how sorry I was, I grabbed my clubs and pulled my nine iron out of my bag. I started to move the club like I would swing it on the course. When I did it, I felt that my wound hurt. Once I realized that I could not get past it and it would most likely open my cut open, I told Paul that I could not go. That made him even more upset.

Like everyone else, Paul started to make a "Good" pot of coffee himself and questioned why I had to cancel. I thought about what happened that caused my injury. So we sat down and I told him that I hurt my shoulder. That basic answer was not good enough.

While I was trying to give a better explanation, Rose came out to the living room. She said, "Scott got into a fight and the guy stabbed him in the back." That would not of been how I would have said it, but now I had to deal with Paul knowing it.

He shook his head and got up to grab us some coffee. Rose sat next to me and put on her shoes. Once she was ready, she walked over to Paul for a hug, then said to us "I am going shopping with my mom. It is good to see you. Sorry, I could not stay longer, but you and Scott can talk without me." Rose was out the door blowing me a kiss while shutting the door.

Now it was only Paul and me left to talk about the elephant that Rose left in the room. It did not take long for Paul to start talking. He was not the kind of man to hide what he meant to say. While he handed me a cup of coffee, he told me not to beat around the bush. I understood that he was telling me to get to the point and tell him what really happened. I did not think he knew of any of the stuff I was doing. That is when I came clean about everything. Paul never judged me, even when I did stupid things. Paul also knew about a lot of stupid things that I did, that I did not know he knew.

"Paul, I should tell you that I sell illegal things. Just wait till I finish, please. But I have done some bad things and one of them was a deal I made recently with some guys that went south. Some of the guys thought they could steal from me, but I had a friend with me. Luckily I came out with only being stabbed in the back." Before I was able to continue with my explanation, Paul yelled at me. He said "What the hell is wrong with you? We taught you not to be this stupid. I heard rumors about you dealing drugs. Now that I know for sure, I don't know what to say. What the hell is wrong with you?" Don't think Paul was trying to verbally beat me down. He only had high hopes for me and he must have felt let down. I felt as I had let him down in a big way.

He started to walk around the apartment. I got up to my feet and started to tell him about how I did not mean for this to happen. I told him how it started and how I got to where I was. Finally, I told Paul about my plan to walk away once Rose was done with school. I thought that he would be happy to hear that. What he heard was that I was going to keep doing things that could get me arrested or killed for another year. It was not as helpful as I figured.

Paul told me to sit down and took his seat as well. We drank our coffee and talked about everything. We even discussed what it would take for me to walk away from everything I was in. I explained to him that I was working on it by teaching someone else how to do what I do. This did not seem to be a good answer. I did not want to tell Paul that there was a good chance if I walked away, I would most likely be killed. Doing it my way might not be the best way, but I knew that I would be alive by the end.

When I first started selling drugs and guns, I romanticized about being the boss. Most people don't think about all the issues that comes with being the boss. There are very few bosses that don't have someone else to answer to. The difference between my type of work and others is that the person I answer to could try to kill me. Now that Paul knows about what I really do and the company people thought I had, it was only a cover, Paul was concerned about me. After several hours of talking and a pot of coffee, it was time for lunch. I made us some sandwiches. They were not fancy, but they worked and once we were done eating, Paul had to go. Before he left, he told me how he doesn't want to see me get hurt or go to prison. With a hug and me telling him that I understand his concerns, he walked out my door. He had to go since he had afternoon plans.

This left me feeling exhausted. I don't think I had anything planned for the rest of the day. Since I had time, I drove around and found myself at a small town ballpark. There was no game being played, but I had the urge to sit on the benches and clear my head. While I sat there thinking, I remembered the promise that I made Duke. I saw a pay phone mounted to the side of a concession stand. I did not want to put it off any longer, so I called John. I did our typical process of calling him and talk to one of his guys. Then I waited for a callback. Since I told the guy I spoke to that I had great news that John would want to know, I got a call from John in about twenty minutes.

When I picked up the ringing phone, I heard "Bearman, this better be good news or I will come to Ohio and teach you why not to toy with me." Well, that was a hell of a way to say hello, at least that was my thought. I told him about the general overview of Mark leaving and selling me his business. While I could hear that he was happy with that news, I said: "Also I need twenty-five thousand for my guy. He is putting together fifty "units" to be sold. This is something I need to do."

Now John was quiet for about a minute until he told me that he will cover that in addition to my next delivery. It dawned on me that it was a total of fifty thousand in counterfeit. John was saying that I need to have an additional fifty thousand on top of my normal exchange. That gave me a week to put my normal package together plus the extra.

I did not want to pass up on this, so I told John that I will get it taken care of. When I finished talking, John made some kind of a grunting sound and hung up. No goodbye, not even a word like a normal person. I had to guess he was having a bad day. I found out later why he was having a bad day. But at that time I did not care.

There was no time to waste to get everything ready. I had to accept that I did not get a full day off. It took me a moment to get myself in gear. Once I did, I drove to Duke's house to find him. I wanted to tell him that we have a deadline to hit. But when I got there, his dad answered the door and said that Duke did not come home yet. I was confused where he might have been as I did not have time to go look for him anymore. I said thank you and got back on the road with a focus on getting to the house.

I wanted to clean everything in the printing room and see if I had everything to make more money, I wanted to start printing. As I was driving, I could only wonder where Duke was. He was gone before I was up and I normally wake up if someone opens my door. The only thing I could figure was that he must have gone to spend time with Jenny. I put it out of my mind and thought about what it would take to get everything done. I remembered that Duke said that we were running low on some supplies. I did not want to spend my day running around finding what we needed. There was a shop that I knew that I could get everything, but I had been warned not to do that. I was told not to get more than two items from a single place as most shops could figure out what you are doing with all the items needed.

By the time I pulled into the driveway, I had every place figured out that was open on a Sunday and I could stock back up. I was proud of myself with figuring out everything in my head. Since it was a very sunny day, I did not notice that the barn cellar door was open till I parked my truck. There were no cars parked at the house. I had to find out what was going on. I shut off my truck and grabbed my gun from my center console. I could not think of any reason that the door should have been opened. The only people who knew about the printing room was Duke, Mick, and myself. My mind was all over the place about why the door was open or who would be down there.

At a fast walking pace, I checked to make sure that my .380 was loaded. When I got about ten yards from the door, Duke walked out. I yelled at him "What the hell?" and he jumped. He almost fell back, but caught himself and yelled back at me. We walked towards each other in the yard, I started asking Duke what he is doing down there and where was his car. Duke went to Jenny's after leaving my place. From what I remembered what he said, Jenny borrowed his car since her car was in the shop. He had Jenny drop him off at the house and he was working since then.

We walked back to the printing room so I could get a list of what was needed and to explain the deal. The basic details that Duke was concerned about was how much he needed to get made with some planning. We figured out that it could be done, it would just take both of us working on it. It was what it was and I agreed that I would get Duke the money for a house. With that in mind, I told Duke that we will get it done. I would have to leave the normal day to day work to Mick while I focused on getting the job done.

Duke and I went over the supplies that we would need. After I had my list together, I started towards my truck when Mick pulled in, which was good since I needed to discuss what is going on. There was no need to put it off and I wanted to see if he felt he could handle it. My other option would be to have him print with Duke and I take care of the daily business dealings. I really wanted to get Mick more into running things while I slowly drifted into the shadows. That would allow me to walk away as I planned.

I yelled at Mick to get his attention. When he looked up, I told him to wait for me. Mick walked onto the porch and sat down. When I got up there to him, he asked what I am doing there, as if I was bothering him. This really did piss me off as I owned the property and he was staying there for free. I also just made him my partner. Now he is being cocky and rude with me. This would not contine to happen as long as I was still there.

"Mick, where do you think you are?" after a moment, I finished with saying "Do you think I am on your property? If after two days of staying here, you think that I need your permission to come here, you are full of shit. I wanted to talk to you about what is going on, but I want to make sure that we are straight about what is going on here." Once I stopped talking, Mick shook his head and apologized to me. He told me that he went back to get more of his stuff, but there was a note on the door. I could easily tell before he told me what was on the note that he saw. The anger that came to his face when he started telling me about the note was the same look on his face the night we ended Jay.

Mick said "The bastard put a note on the door saying my stuff was in the yard. When I went to see where he put it, I found my clothes in a trash bag next to the burn barrel. In the barrel was some of my stuff that he had already burned. There were empty bottles all over the place. I found parts of my things, but nothing could be saved. I found some of my pictures. I only grabbed my clothes." He looked as if he was about to tear up. I wanted to say something helpful, but I did not have anything good to say. The only thing I could do was get up and walk out to my truck. I reached under my passenger seat where I keep my personal supply of weed and rolled a joint. Once I was finished, I gave the paper a lick and went back to Mick.

We smoked the joint without saying a word until we were halfway through. Mick thanked me for listening and just sitting. Then on his next exhale, he asked me what I wanted to talk to him about. Since he was ready to talk about other things, I started to explain the deal I made with John. I told him how Duke was going to ask Jenny to marry him. After everything had been explained to Mick about what would be needed, he said it would not be a problem.

To my shock, Mick told me that he believed I was pushing more on him. When he confronted me about this while we were sitting there, I had no way to get around it. I told him all my plans about eventually having him take over completely once I have enough money. We discussed how my timeline was six to eight months down the road and what I was going to do once I left. Mick became a little happier with learning this. I told him that I did not care if he starts acting like he was the boss, as long as he remembers who was in charge until I was gone. He agreed and with a handshake, I was off to get my shopping done.

It did not take me long to get everything on the list. I even had plenty of time to stop and get a bite to eat. Most likely, I would be there an hour before Duke needed me. It seemed that everything was coming together. Now that Mick was aware of what my exit plan was, I believed that it would make things much easier. I found out that sometimes you need to make sure everyone involved knows what they can and can't do. The littlest mistake could make thing much harder.

As for that day, I spent a good part of the day trying to explain what I do so Paul understood. Then I made a deal with John and got Mick on board with my plans. I knew that Mark was leaving in a few weeks and that would leave us with no competition to speak of. We had our product lines spreading to more cities and having more stock come in. If I keep everything up like that, I could have become the main supplier for Ohio. That thought made me chuckle as I knew that it would not happen and I was good with that. I was excited about all this.

When I got back to the house, Duke was on the porch with Mick. I was confused as it should have taken him longer to get everything ready for me. When I got out of the truck and grabbed the boxes of supplies Mick yelled: "I got you a new bottle." I could see the red wax seal and squarish shaped bottle. I figured that Mick was in a good mood after being told I am moving everything to him. They both seem to be in a good mood and I figured that we all had something to celebrate.

I carried the boxes up to the porch where they were sitting and joined them for a couple of drinks. By the time I put down the boxes Mick already had a glass of Maker's Mark poured and ready for me. I was very content to be able to relax and sit and talk. To my surprise, Duke ended up telling me that Mick was telling him that he was going to be the boss soon. This just ruined my time to drink. I ended up telling Mick that telling people will end up screwing things up for me. I also told him it might possibly get me killed. I explained as well if John heard that I was leaving he would end up killing me by himself. I explained to Mick that I just needed to get everything set up so that John wouldn't care and still had money coming in.

Mick said he understood and I believed that he did. I know Mick didn't want me dead as we got along too well for that. I nodded and let it go and then we went back to drinking. I had a nice glass of Makers Mark or maybe two. We talked about our stories and Mick said that he was told by Duke that he was going to ask Jenny to marry him. We all laughed and teased him about it. By the time we finished the sun was already setting. It was time for me to go home and see if Rose made it back yet.

The drive home didn't seem like it was as long as normal. I don't know if I was speeding or if my mind was just off someplace else, but before I knew it I was home. Either way, when I got home I saw Rose's car which made me even happier. I shut off my truck and went into my place, and saw Rose cooking dinner for us.

I asked Rose what she's cooking for dinner and how did she knew I'd actually be home in time for dinner to begin with. She smiled and said she's getting ready for whenever I actually did come home. It seems like she was being nice and trying to make sure that I was well fed. So I went to grab a beer out of the fridge and I saw that she also went grocery shopping. To my amazement, everything was filled up and there was not an empty spot in the fridge.

It was a surprise to me to see that she did this. Rose knew she didn't have to, but when I told her this, she gave me a big hug and a kiss and I asked her why she did it. Rose turned away, saying that if she was going to live here she needed to make sure we have plenty of food. That threw me off and I asked her what she meant. Rose explained to me that she spent the day with her mom discussing her living with me. They agreed that she spends all her time at my place and we were engaged. It only made sense that she completely moved in. I did not see her mom going for this too quickly.

Her moving in did not make a difference for us. With as much as Rose stayed with me, I considered that she was already living with me. She just had a different mailing address. That is what I thought until I walked into the bedroom. That is when I saw all of my shirts on the bed and a new dresser. The room looked like Rose was storing everything that she owned in there. Now the big dinner made sense. But as it might have stressed me without any notice, I was still happy that Rose did it. When she completely moved in, my worries went away.

After dinner, we started to figure out where to put her stuff and what could I get rid of to make some more room. I had a lot of old clothes, a lot of my jeans that had holes in them. Rose was happy to see them go since she hated them. You can guess that what got put in a bag was meant for goodwill. Rose joked about how we need to go shopping and replace my pants. Maybe Rose was waiting for this, as she did hate a lot of my old clothes. Only she knows if she was planning this or if it was just a happy accident. Either way, she got her way. She got her way till about midnight as she went through my clothes to decide what I should keep or donate. Once we were done, we both were tired and fell asleep on the bed fully dressed.

Chapter Fourteen

A few months had passed since that weekend. The summer was coming to an end and Mark had already left. I handed the cash to him and we had a nice talk before he left. Shortly after that, Duke had asked Jenny to marry him. In case you were wondering, she did say yes and they are discussing moving to Texas after Jenny will finish school. I got the money that I promised for him. It had been quiet since then. I even reached out to the guys in Detroit, but they made it clear that we would not be doing any kind of business together. That was OK with Mick and me too. We had a good chunk of the drug business in Toledo and we were working with a gang up there. They also would buy the random guns that we got from John. Everything was going good for us.

Then things started to change with the littlest details. It started when Mick came to me after doing an exchange with one of John's guys. Mick said that the driver was talking about how he kept seeing the same two cars for most of the drive. It seemed to freak out Mick because he said that he thought people would follow him every now and again. I hoped that Mick was being paranoid. In case he was not, I needed to figure out what was going on.

Once I had a chance, I went to find a payphone. I left messages for the local mayors and cops that I had on my payroll. I got nervous when the Fremont Chief of Police answered my call. He said that he cannot discuss an ongoing investigation. He followed up with saying a phrase I use to say to cops that I paid. He said, "A single lit match can cause a lot of damage." This meant to tell me that something or someone was working to destroy what I built. He hung up and I did not worry about getting a call back from any of the others. I had a feeling that I would not hear from them. It would make sense that they had heard something or were trying to work with whoever is coming after me. I know that it did not make any difference who it was, but I really wanted to know.

I started to pay attention more to what cars were around me. This was not what I needed, but over the next few days, I did not see anyone following me. Some of the guys have told Mick that they keep seeing cops in their neighborhoods more than usual. Mick said that the car following him was not good at hiding it. I guess it is hard to follow someone in the country. Most of the time, you could drive between a few towns and not see anyone else driving. When you see the same car going everywhere you go, you know that they are following you. I did not know why I was not followed at that time. Maybe those people know everything they need to about me. If that is the case, they might be trying to get one of my guys to turn on me.

When Friday came around, Rose and Jenny had made plans for us to go to one of their friend's house. I don't remember what we were going to do, but I remember it was raining and thundering. Every thunder strike felt like a shotgun being fired behind me. Jenny and Duke showed up at our place so we all could go together. When they ran in the door, a loud bang of thunder cracked again. Rose said that their friend called and canceled. She was fighting with her boyfriend again and would not see anyone. We all were still ready to go out, so I called a restaurant in Tiffin that Duke and Rose kept talking about. The restaurant said that they were not busy and we could walk in and grab a table.

With that news, we all ran to my truck trying to avoid each raindrop and failing at the attempt. It was a fun trip with listing to the radio and listening to the girls singing along, and even Duke and I joined in a few time. When we were on County Road 592 coming up to route 53, I turned down the sound to the radio. I had to ask if anyone had noticed anything strange in the last week or two. Since Duke had told Jenny that he was making money by making money, I was not worried about saying anything in front of her. At that point, Duke and I both did not do much with the business. We did more consulting. That way we could walk away and not worry.

Duke said that Mick asked him the same thing and told him that he was being followed. When the girls heard this, they started to get concerned. Their first thought went to another dealer trying to get in and might be like Jay with his tactics. That was not even a thought, but I don't think that would be the case. If it was, the Chief would not have said what he did. I explained that I thought it might be something like a DEA or FBI type of people. I told them that we might have nothing to worry about since we have not seen anything. The girls relaxed, but Duke looked as he was trying to act as he was not concerned. I saw his eyes and I knew that he had more questions.

When we got to the restaurant, the girls ran to the bathroom to straighten up. They were off before we were even seated at our table. Once they were off, Duke asked me what I really thought about what is going on. I owed him the truth. "Duke, I think we don't see anyone because they already know about us or me. You hang around me a lot. Only Mick and I know you print for us." Then before I got to say anything more, he reminded me that Dan knew about it too.

Well crap, I forgot about him. Dan has not been around since

Ferris left. I started to wonder if he got in trouble for something and turned on us. It would not surprise me that he would do something like that. Now I wish I would have caught up with him after he tried to betray me the last time. Maybe if I taught him that it is a damaging action to one's health to talk to the wrong people. Knowing Dan, I don't know if it would.

I must have got lost in my thoughts. Duke grabbed my arm so we could follow a sweet older lady saying something about being our waitress. We sat across from each other at an old round beat up table. I told Duke that he was done with the printing. If someone comes to him, don't add anything, but know that they know about me already. I suggested that he makes a deal to save himself and hide any cash that he already had. I wanted to start being more cautious. As I noticed that Duke did not feel any better, I guessed that he was not encouraged when I told him to sell me out. The fact is, if they know about him, they know about me. I had considered this being something that could happen. It was a thought after the first day I sold an ounce of weed and some cocaine to a guy in Fostoria.

I would need to make sure that John did not get the idea that I was selling him out. This was something I did not think I would have to think about when I started. Other than getting arrested, I figured the worst thing that would happen would be a beating. Now that I had to worry about going to prison and being killed, it did not feel like I had an easy solution. As I said, well crap. I would have to put all this out of my mind as the girls had joined Duke and me at the table. Rose is asking what I want and telling me what not to get, in case she wants to try my food.

The girls seem to not think about anything that we talked about on the way to the restaurant. I know Rose and Jenny both were told that they would need to remember not to tell people what we do. We told them if anyone asks about what Duke and I do, they should tell them that we are brokers. If they want more details, the girls could tell them that we were crop brokers. This way they don't get involved in anything that might ever happen.

I ended up ordering something that Rose wanted and I ate what she ordered for herself. She did not like her order, so we switched plates. This was not the first time we have done this. I figured this is how I learned to eat what was put in front of me. Jenny and Duke were talking between each other most of the dinner. It was a good night and I was trying to not think about what could be coming.

We walked out of the restaurant, and the rain had stopped and there were puddles everywhere. We were being stupid by jumping over the big puddles and laughing. We laughed harder when someone did not make it or when anyone about fell. Watching us, you would think we had been drinking. At least that was what the guys sitting in a car at the other end of the parking lot must have thought. I don't know if I was being paranoid, but I thought that was the first time I saw that I was being watched. This did not make me feel well as I knew that someone was following me.

I did not like that my personal life was being watched. My stomach started to turn with me wondering how close they were to coming and arresting me. I kept looking in the rear-view mirror as we went down Route 53 on our way back to my place. I noticed that the car was following me, but was about two miles behind me. When I saw the drive-in theater coming up I prepared to turn. I came up with an idea to see if I could get a better look at the guys following me.

When I turned onto County Road 592, I asked everyone if they felt something. They looked at each other and said they felt nothing. When I saw the car turn on the road with us, I told everyone that I was going to stop and look to make sure I did not hit something. With being in the country, this was not something that is out of the ordinary. I turned on my four ways and pulled to the side of the road. I grabbed a flashlight and my .380 from my center console. The girls asked why I was grabbing my gun, but I quickly answered saying that I don't want to have something suffer if I had hit it.

By the time I got out of my truck and put my gun in my back pocket, the car pulled up to me. They stopped to ask if I needed help. These guys were dressed too nice to be from the country. The driver was a blonde guy who looked as if he does not get out during the day much. The passenger was brown-haired who seemed angry as his general mood. These guys did not come across as some fellas from any of the farm towns in Northwestern Ohio. They were too old to be college kids, and too many fast food bags on the floor to be from around there.

When they pulled up to me, I turned my flashlight on. I acted as I was looking around my tires and walked up to my front bumper. The blonde guy yelled over his passenger asking "Everything OK? Do you need any help?" The passenger looked as he was trying to smile for the first time in his life. They got out of their car and they both were about six foot something. They stood a bit taller than me, so I used that to my advantage. I made myself seem smaller and as harmless as I could. I wanted them to think that I was not the type of guy that had the balls to do anything worse than speeding. John used to tell me it's easier to take someone that underestimated you.

As we were looking around my truck, I handed the flashlight to the brown-haired guy. He kneeled down and looked under my truck. While he did that, I saw that he had a gun shoved in the back of his jeans. I figured screw it and asked about it. So I said; "Wow, what kind of gun is that? We only carry rifles and shotguns around here." He got up very quickly when realizing that he forgot that he had his gun back there. The blonde guy answered as quickly as his friend got up with "Oh, we carry because you don't know what is out here." They did not like that I started to laugh.

"So what are you guys, cops or feds? Locals know a handgun will not be the best choice for the coyotes that are out here. You would be best to keep a short barrel shotgun." As I was saying this and making my statement, they started walking back to their car. Then they drove away without saying anything. I would have to guess feds because local cops liked to tell people they were cops. It gave them a power trip and most people my age would get nervous around them. I had to guess that only feds had to be that rude. Even cops would say have a good day.

When I got into my truck, Rose asked me what was that all about. She wanted to know why those guys walked around the way they did. It might have not been the best answer, but I said that they are my new friends. All my friends take time to warm up to me. Rose said in a tone that meant we will talk about this later "OK". I knew that she would not let it go, but she did not want to push with Jenny and Duke there. We went back to having a good night. Duke and Jenny were distracting each other in the back seat, so it was easy to act like nothing was wrong.

We were the only ones on the road the rest of the way back to my place. Rose and Jenny began to talk about plans for what they wanted to do next. While I was listening, I felt Duke tap my shoulder. I saw him holding a cigarette already lit between the seats. Rose took it from him and took a hit from it before giving it to me. Duke and Jenny went crazy about Rose doing that because they have never seen her smoke. The truth was that she did not smoke. She would have one while drinking with me or take a hit once and awhile like she had that night. I would have guessed that she did it to get a rise out of the other two.

I lost track of what was being said over the laughing, although it was fun . I decided to go through the village of Risingsun. I wanted to go to a drive–thru on route 23. They did not care what age you were, as long as you had cash. The old guy who owned it always had a simple rule, tell him it was for your parents or he would not sell you anything. It was one of those little secrets that only the locals knew. It was not the best–looking place, but I had a feeling that the old guy was running his own little side weed business. I always wondered if he was growing and selling. He was high a lot. I knew he was at least selling since I had some guys tell me. I never got to ask him because that was the last time I saw him. I got a case of bud light and finished our drive back home.

We finished the night off sitting around and drinking some beers. It was not like we drank so much that I had a hangover, but I did get a sinus headache when I woke up. It was that time of the year. It was around ten at night when Duke and I stepped out for a smoke. While we were out there, he did not wait to ask me who the guys in the car were. I guess he was paying more attention than I thought he was. I told him that I was thinking that they were feds, maybe the FBI. I explained they were not locals and they had guns on them. It was kind of a joke to me that it was like something I saw on a TV cop show and perhaps I didn't take it too seriously.

Duke started to show how worried he was now as he kept talking about what he was going to do. I told him that I think I know what needs to be done, but it will not end well for me. When he asked me what I was talking about, I reminded him of our discussion with John when he was in town a while ago. Still confused, I reminded Duke of our plan in case of things headed south from what we were going to do. By the time I finished my smoke, he had remembered what I was talking about. He was not happy about it and said: "Is there another way, I thought we were past that." Duke took the last hit of his cigarette and said "Well crap, I hoped that it would never have come to that. I did not think about the FBI getting involved. Let keep this to us. The girls don't need to know."

Then as he was about to ask me more about it, Jenny walked out to tell us to come back in because they want to play a board game. For some reason, the girls love to play board games while we drank and it was just the four of us. We all sat around the table and Rose had Monopoly set up. We play these games enough that we all knew what each other preferred to play as. Rose had the battleship for me, the hat for Duke, the iron for Jenny, and Rose always took the guy on the horse. When it was only the four of us and no one was watching, we like to be nerdy. There was no pressure to be any other way and we could be eighteen/nineteen years old.

While we were in the middle of the game and the girls worked together to take Duke and me out, Duke said he heard some news. As he said it, I rolled and landed on Kentucky Ave. where Jenny had a hotel on it. That took me out with a thousand fifty rental fee and only a few hundred in my hand. I pretended as if I was upset that I lost, but it was not a big deal to me. Once I was done acting and making a foolish scene, I asked Duke what he heard. It caught me off guard when he said that Riggs left for boot camp last week.

I remembered that Riggs was going to the Marines. I thought he would say a final goodbye after everything that happened. It would have been nice to talk with him and wish him luck. I guess I shouldn't have been surprised since he said that he would not be coming around me. His mom felt that I was to blame for Dan and Riggs' action, more focus on the actions that put them in the hospital. I missed Riggs, but I only wished him luck on everything, even if he didn't know it.

Rose and Jenny started joking about Riggs in boot camp. They were picturing him being yelled at by a drill Sargent. When Duke said that we should watch Stripes, we all started laughing. We joked about Riggs being Russell. It was no longer sad that Riggs was gone, but every time any of us thought of Riggs, you would hear "Russell". As for the rest of the night, it went as any other night did.

The only difference was when I went out to smoke after I lost all my money in Monopoly. When I stood outside, before looking around, I lit my cigarette. Once I closed my zippo, I saw a car sitting across the street. I knew it was the same guys from earlier. I did not want to have Duke or either of the girls see them. I chose to go talk to them and ask if they would park a bit down the street.

When I got to their car, the driver rolled down his window. He did not even put up any act this time. I started to tell them that I don't know why they are following and watching me. If they would park a quarter mile down the street, there is a gravel road they could sit and not be seen. I let my cocky side show a bit and I blew smoke into their car. I suggested the other option would be for me to call the state troopers. Talking about the troopers must have been what got them to move out of sight. From what I always read in different books and saw in the movies, the FBI would work with the local cops. It seemed that they want to keep the local cops out of their way. They seem to never mention anything about the state police. I hoped that these guys would not question if the troopers were part of what they were doing.

As I saw them pull onto the gravel road, I flicked my cigarette on the road and went back in to join everyone. The game was wrapping up with only Rose and Duke left, and Jenny in the kitchen making a snack for us. We finished a good night with some talking and listening to Duke. He joked about how Rose only beat him because she cheated. There is nothing like nights like that night when you don't have to be the one that people look up to or fear. I got love from my friends and Rose.

By the morning, Jenny and Duke were somehow both sleeping on the couch. Even though Duke slept on the outside and looked as he was holding on for dear life so as not to fall off. This was not the first time they have slept like that, but it made me chuckle when I saw it. I knew that I should have woken everyone up since they all had something planned, but I was in the mood to make pancakes. No one ever left when I was making pancakes with cinnamon sugar and vanilla.

When I got to the point to put them on the Griddle, Rose came out started to remind me that I should have woke them up. She started to give Duke a little shake of the shoulder. That is when Rose screamed and jumped back. The next thing I heard was a thud on the floor and Duke saying some choice words. That also woke Jenny up, so two birds down with one stone. I thought of making a joke about it but kept my mouth shut.

Duke got up off the floor, looked in the kitchen and asked what I was making. I said that I was making pancakes. He did not wait till I finished making all the pancakes. He grabbed the plates from the cabinet and started to set up everything for us to eat together. Then he found out what the girls wanted to drink. By the time I finished the last pancake and turned around with the plate, everyone sat ready. They had their drinks, plates, and Duke even had my black coffee ready for me.

Duke and Jenny talked about how they had to go to his grandma's house for a family lunch they were doing. Rose and I were invited, but Rose already had plans to go spend the day with her dad in Findlay and I was not invited to that. Her dad hated me, but I did not blame him. It made sense that no father would like a guy that is with his daughter. Every dad knows what they did when younger and they expect other boys to do the same things. That is why my day was open with nothing planned.

While we were discussing our day, Rose asked what I was going to do for the day. I said that there were a few people that I would visit and I might stop by Jerry's Tattoos in Fremont. I mentioned that I wanted to look at getting something to cover the scar on my back. That brought up all sorts of discussion. We talked about what kind of tattoo everyone wanted for themselves. We also talked about what they thought I should be getting. At the end of breakfast, I decided that I would get a Celtic cross.

Although the tattoo was a reason to go to the tattoo shop, it was not the main reason. There was a guy who worked out of that tattoo shop that also made new identities. I first met the guy when I needed a fake ID and I had kept in touch with him since then. He had been working at the tattoo shop for about a year.

Jenny and Duke cleaned up after breakfast was done. They giggled and teased each other as if they had just started to date. Rose was in the shower getting ready to go to meet her dad. With everyone doing something, I went out to have a smoke. When I did, I saw those guy's car sitting behind a tree on the graveled road. I stood there looking at them while I smoked and Duke came out to join me.

"Is that the same guys from last night?" Duke asked as he lit his cigarette. I told him that it was and I talked with them while they were playing Monopoly. Duke wanted to know if they would be doing anything. My best guess was they were trying to get more information on me and that is what I told Duke. I told him that I would suggest he hide the gun I gave him and any weed he might have.

Jenny came outside and asked Duke if he was ready. Jenny

went down the stairs and Duke slapped me on the back. He said that everything will be OK and he had a good feeling. He joined Jenny in the car and they were on their way. I finished my cigarette and went in where Rose was in the living room. She was on the couch putting on her shoes. I sat next to her and asked when she would be home. The truth was that I did not have much to do since I turned a lot over to Mick.

Rose told me she was going to spend the day with her dad and would be back around eight. I kissed her and told her I will look forward to her getting home. With that, Rose was out the door and on her way to Findlay. Now I had to figure out what to do with my day. The tattoo shop did not open until one in the afternoon.

As I sat down and finished off my coffee, I decided to go talk with Mick. With me being followed, I wanted to let him know what I was planning. If things go as I figured they would, Mick would need to be included and hopefully save himself. It took me a few minutes to find my travel mug that I use for coffee. I did not want to mix my wine travel mug and coffee travel mug. I have tasted coffee wine in my life once and I am glad it was only once. I had no interest in mixing them before or after that tasting.

A full mug of coffee and a half–full pack of cigarettes in hand, I was out the door. As I went down the stairs, I noticed that my new friends had left. I did not expect that to be the last time I saw them, but I was not going to wait for them to return. On that note, I was on my way down the road and took a different route. I wanted to make sure that I was not being followed. It only took me an extra ten minutes to get to the house.

Mick had not moved out and had no plans to move out. He had fixed up the house to make it a nice place to live. He even had a guy who would cut the grass for some weed in return. I no longer just walked into the house, even though I still owned it. I knocked on the door and he came to the door in his boxers. It was clear that I woke him up, but I did not care. Once he had opened the door, he stepped out of my way and I went into the living room and sat on a La-Z-Boy chair.

As I sat on the chair, I asked if he just got a bunch of new furniture. He smiled and told me that he got a good deal for it. He only had to give two thousand dollars for everything. That is when it dawned on me why we had been watched. Mick was spending money more than he should have. To fix up the house was not cheap, the furniture was paid for in cash, and he had been improving his car. He was trying to make his car a muscle car. He had drawn attention by doing what I told him not to do.

I followed up with telling him that I am now being followed. He sat down and asked what we had to do. Mick still depended on me for advice and some big decisions. I was beginning to wonder how he would keep things running when I was gone. It did not matter to me in the long run and I had to remember that. I got it out of my head and told him that we will first have to come up with a reason that he had the money. People may ask how he was able to pay to do everything he was doing. I took it that he never asked why I hid my money instead of spending when I made it. I had to explain it to him that people will watch what others spend their money on. Those same people will talk, which will get to people you would not want it to.

Mick asked me who would say anything since no one sees the house as he was fixing it up. I could not help but to shake my head. I kept making motions to say that he did not understand what I was getting at. I went into details to tell him that people drive by and we have people who don't like us and want to get rid of us. I reminded him that some cops don't accept our money. That is what it took to turn on the light bulb for him

"Do you know what I think? I think Dan might have said something. I think he wants to get even with me for not letting him cut us out of our business." This comment to Mick seemed to upset him as I figured it would. We talked about it more and I explained what I needed him to do. One thing was not to touch Dan. I wanted to deal with him, if I could. I told Mick if I can't get to Dan, he can go after him.

Mick did not like the end results of my plan, but he understood that it was necessary. While I was picking up my truck key, Mick said that he will cut out the spending. I thanked him and left to finish getting things done.

Going down the road, I had to figure out what I was going to do since I had just under a year before Rose and I were out of Ohio. I was hoping that I made it that long. I was questioning if I would with these new issues of the police or most likely the feds coming after me. That is why I decided to go for a tattoo. I meant to get my new documents and to have a new life back when I was fighting with the Himlees. I was taught that you should always have a backup plan. This was the backup plan and I was hoping that it did not come to it.

To be honest, I was scared to have to use my backup plan. Getting these documents made had me realizing that things were closer to possibly needing to leave everything behind. As I drove into Fremont and down State Street, I wonder if I could manage to leave everything. I was wondering if it would be better to go to jail and get out so I could just be with Rose afterward. If all else failed, I could just have a normal life and start over after.

When I was only about three blocks from the tattoo shop, I got pulled over by a regular marked cop. I was not thrilled since I did not do anything, plus I was not sure if Mick was making the payments as he was supposed to do. When the cop got up to my door, I realized Mick had made the last payment. The cop asked for my driver license and registration. When I reached into my glove box for the registration, I heard the cop tell me to "Keep my head covered". I did not realize that the guy was one of mine, but I was glad. I handed him my registration and asked who it was that is checking into me.

He did not answer and walked back to his car to check my record. Luckily I was a good driver most of the time and did not have anything on my record. When I say nothing, I had never even had a parking ticket on my record. That is why the cop came back and said he was giving me a warning. Then said that the DEA or FBI will not be as nice. He drove off, leaving me there with that information. I could not sit in the road thinking about it, so I drove the final three blocks.

When I walked into Jerry's Tattoos, I saw Ryan in the back in the doorway. Ryan was a big guy who did the documents that I needed and tattoos. When the guy at the counter asked if he could help me, I said I was there to see Ryan and have him do some work for me. He walked back and talked to him. They acted like I could not see them, even though they stood in the doorway as they talked. Ryan went into the room I assumed was the one he was renting. The guy from the counter came back asking me to sit down to wait for him. What was else was I going to do? I sat looking around wondering why tattoo shops painted the walls black or a dark purple.

I did not plan to get an answer about the walls. Ryan had me wait long enough to come up with another pointless question. He had me come back to his room where he had a drafting table set up with drawings all over. He seems to be very busy doing tattoos. We discussed the cross I wanted on my back to cover the scar and why I did not want anyone to have any copies of the cross when he was done. He looked confused about that request until I said that I also need papers and an ID.

I about crapped myself when he said it would be ten grand and it did not help that he said that includes the tattoo. When I asked him why so much, he said that he had to pay a buddy. His buddy worked turning everything digital for the Ohio state government. I could only guess that his buddy was going to make my new information get into the system. I took what he was telling me that my new identity would be able to be searched as if my new person had always been around.

We shook hands and I went to leave when he asked what name I wanted. I thought for a moment till I said I could go with Nathaniel Norris and it better be a hell of a tattoo. That took care of everything I needed to do for the day. With nothing to do, I decided to go spend time with my mom and Paul.

Chapter Fifteen

More than a week had past when Ryan called me and said he had everything ready for my tattoo. I set up a time for me to go in and I was excited with it being my first tattoo. When I told Rose, she decided she would come with me when I got the work done. She was excited to see it done and even considered getting one too. I did not want anyone to come with me, as I did not want anyone to know what I was doing. I had a few days to figure it out and take care of it.

I was thinking about what to do so I did not raise any questions from Rose. I got lost in my own thoughts again until Rose Started to talk. It felt like I was in my head a lot lately. Rose was telling me about how she wanted to go to meet up with her friends at Oogie's in Gibsonburg. Oogie's was a pizza place that we used to go to. I liked their porky pig subs and figured it would be nice to be around some different people. Plus I got along with the staff there. So, I smiled and told her how I thought it would be a good time. I had met those people before, but they never gave me much attention. I always took it as they did not like me much, but they would treat me nicely if I was around.

We decided that we were going to go for a walk before we met with her friends. Why not as it was a perfect looking day and the sun was setting leaving a hint of daylight. We did not have the sun beating down on us. I remember that we parked next to the railroad tracks and we were across the street from the police station. I don't know why, but I always love to park by the police. It felt like an inside joke that the police did not know.

We walked down the road to the park. It was not much more than an open grassy area and a baseball diamond. We liked to walk around it because that was where we first met. She and Jenny were running around being a bit goofy as was normal for them during a fair that was going on. I remember that it was after Sara had left and I went to the fair to meet up with a cousin who I had not seen in a long time. That is when I saw Jenny and we got to talking. Then Rose came up to have Jenny go on some ride with her. I felt something right then, but I did not say anything. The three of us walked around till I ran into my cousin and his friends. The girls went their way and I went mine. I was hoping that we did not find my cousin, but we did.

I saw Rose around a few time after that in the following months then Jenny and Duke set us up on a date. It was easy to see what they were doing when we showed up but Duke and

Jenny never did. We talked and hung out for a few hours that night. That is how Rose got to know the side of me that no one else had. We joked about how she gave me a hard time the first time she met me.

There was no reason for us to rush to get to the restaurant. We walked around and fooled around in the baseball dugout just to have some fun. We walked around the outside of the baseball fields fence until we came to the back corner. It was next to the railroad tracks. I had forgotten that Cameron had a buddy who lived on a dirt alley on the other side of the tracks. I was reminded of this because he was on the porch drinking when he saw me walking with Rose.

I heard "Scott, I am going to deal with you right now." Rose and I turned to see Cameron coming down the steps of his buddies place looking at me. I told Rose to go to the restaurant and wait for me. I did not want her to be around for what was going to happen next. She knew about Cameron's past with me and how abusive he could get. So Rose listened to me and walked on. Before I knew it, Cameron was grabbing my shirt and pulling me towards him.

Dirt and grass were all I could see as I fell to the ground and felt a shin hit the side of my chest. Cameron was not an overly heavy guy, but he knew how to put the weight that he had into a hit. I tried to push through the pain to grab his leg on the next kick, but his buddy came from the other side and picked me up. I heard the bastard make a comment about how I was on my own this time. My best guess was that Cameron told him a story that matched some story he made up. I could only imagine that it was something to make him look good. Now add some beers and hyping each other up. I just turned into a can of gas that got poured onto a fire.

When I was on my feet and being restrained by Cameron's buddy, I saw Cameron's fist coming. It was not the first time as I believed I have mentioned that he did this kind of stuff, but that did not make it hurt any less. It reminded me that it doesn't matter how big, tough, or feared you might be. When it comes to pain, none of that matters. I felt everything done to me and it hurt like hell. That was the worst that had been done to me up to that point. Sadly, I have taken some beatings. That helped me deal with fighting people my size.

I was not too clear on things by the end of it, but the police showed up and stopped them from doing anything more to me. They were arrested and the police took pictures of me once I was off the ground. I don't remember how I got to the hospital, but I was told that Rose came with her friends that we were going to meet up with. By the time I was thinking clearly and able to focus, I was laid out on a bed with curtains all around the bed. My mom, Paul, and Rose were standing there by my side.

I started to ask what had happened when the doctor walked in. The guy did not even look at me but kept his eyes on his clipboard. From what he said, I had several bruised bones and a fractured rib. He went on to tell me that I could not drink any alcohol with the pain meds he was putting me on. I could only imagine he was going to prescribe OxyContin or oxycodone. Those were a common pill I would have got from John. They were also very popular when we got them.

The doctor looked up to me when he wanted to know if I had any questions. Before I got to say anything, my mom asked a few questions and talked to Rose about everything when the doctor left. It was almost as they did not remember I was there. I didn't care at that moment. I hurt all over and I felt sleepy. I was only thinking about getting home and try to heal.

It took about an hour for the doctor to sign his name on some form that allowed me to leave. I could see how high I was on his list, but what did I expect. He did not know me and would never see me again. As far as he must have been concerned, I was some punk kid that got my ass kicked.

As soon as the doctor did sign the form, we were out the door and the four of us went to my place. Paul was making jokes to help break the mood. One of his jokes got me to laugh and oh did my side hurt. The car ride was not too much fun, but I got home where I saw my truck, Jenny's car, and Mick's car too. I knew that

I would have a full house for a bit. It made sense that they would be there if they heard what happened. Rose told me she called Duke to have him bring back my truck. He must have called Mick and went to Jenny's where he parked his car. Then he would of went to get my truck to bring it to my place.

It was good to see my friends coming to see me only because they wanted to make sure I was OK. Paul helped me up my stairs and the pain made me make sounds that Paul mistook for laughing. I was not laughing, but it made him laugh. I could see Paul was concerned about me. The funny thing was, I figured that out of everyone I knew, Paul would be the one to go kick Cameron's ass for what he did to me. I don't think he ever did, but they never were anywhere near each other. My mom might have also calmed him down after they left my place.

They did not leave right away, once we got into the door, Duke and Mick came to help Paul with me. We talked for about half an hour before my mom and Paul left. My mom mainly kept asking if I was going to press charges. I said I would, but I most likely would not. I doubted that it would do anything more then put me in a public view I did not want.

When it was Mick, Duke, Jenny, Rose, and myself, Rose gave me more details of what happened. She ran to the police station and told them what was happening. That is why they showed up, but they did not hurry to get to me. Considering how bad I was beaten up, I will never believe that those cops wanted to do anything as they were in eyesight of where I was being beaten up. I also could have been wrong and they knew about my reputation. That could be the reason they did not rush to help me.

It was either Duke or Mick who made the joke; "if we are going to be followed around, you would have thought that they would have helped." And it was good for a short laugh, but I started to wonder where they were. If the guys following me saw that I was being beaten by Cameron like that, they would have gotten the police or helped. Instead, they either were not around for once, or they just sat there and watched. What really bothered me was what if they did stop following me. What does that mean? I popped a pain killer and drank my beer. It was a lite beer, so it was not anything to worry about, at least that's what I told myself.

By the time ten o'clock came around, everyone was finally going out the door. There were still things that needed done. The difference for me was that I could not do anything. I had to lay on my couch and rest. Rose would not leave my side other than to get something for us to eat and drink. Rose and I watched some TV for the rest of the night. There was not much on TV, but it was all we had to do. When it was time for us to sleep, I remained on the couch while Rose went into the bedroom. I did not sleep much because every turn I made woke me up.

Rose came out to check on me before she got around in the morning. She was surprised to see me in the Kitchen. I had already had a pot of coffee made and was cleaning up. It was not a fast process of cleaning, but it was done. Rose yelled at me and asked "What the hell is wrong with you?" the little sleep I was running on allowed me to think it would be a good idea to joke with a list of bad habits I had. Let's say that she did not find the same humor as I did. Once she was done with letting me know how upset she was, she walked into the bedroom to get around to go to school. Since she started her senior year, I always heard how happy life would be once June came around.

I had put my cup on the counter and started to pour myself some coffee when Rose came out. She grabbed a bowl of cereal for her breakfast. I promised her that I would be OK and I would take it easy. After explaining to her that I would not be driving, but I had to get used to the pain as much as I could. I did not want it to stop me from getting things done. She basically said OK, but clearly indicated that she would show me what real pain was if I hurt myself worst. I believed her too. Who do you think taught me what happens when you hit someone with open hands on both ears.

She was off and I was alone. I had to lay down because the pain was getting worse. I took another pill and worked my way to shower. I needed to clean up since I had not been able to since we left to go to Oogie's the day before. I felt dirty and could not stand it any longer. During the shower, I accepted that nothing I was going to do would be done in a hurry, at least not if I wanted to avoid unnecessary pain. Once I was done showering, I did not worry about getting dressed and walked around with just my towel. That made it kind of an odd situation when I came out of the bedroom and saw someone sitting in my living room.

Not to be rude to whoever this guy was, I offered him coffee. He stood up and held out a cup saying "I could use another cup." The guy looked down at me by about six inches and walked to the kitchen as though I was the guest in his home. He did not have much of a tan but was not too pale. For some reason, he was not rushing to tell me who he was or why he was there.

When I grabbed the pot of coffee, I felt a sharp pain and realized that I could not watch him and put coffee in the cups. The guy must have realized this too because he came around to my side of the kitchen island. He poured us both some coffee and went back to the other side of the island. Then sat on one of the seats while I remained standing on my side. I was trying to remember if I had anything in reach to protect myself.

We did not take our eyes off of each other while we sipped our coffee in silence. I got tired of it and asked him who he was. He seemed to be happy to answer me. Smiling when he said; "I am Tom Stone. I was wondering how long it would take for you to ask." I followed up with the next question saying "Tom, why are you in my place? I don't imagine that you came in here to watch me walk around in a bath towel."

Tom did confirm that he did not come to see me in a towel and he really wanted me to put on some pants. I also let him know that I was not moving from where I was. Not till I knew why there was a stranger in my place. Another minute passed of us looking at each other across the island, and he started to explain what he was doing in my place. There was something about the way Tom talked that I could not place where he was from.

He said that he was with a company acting as a middle man. He was there to help me with my problem. I first thought he was someone coming to talk to me about Cameron. I figured that he might have been a lawyer to see what I was going to do. I knew that Cameron had a buddy who had a law partner in a firm located in downtown Toledo. I prepared myself for him to threaten me or any other tactics. That is until the guy said he knew John, which quickly got my attention.

"John who? I know a John that works at a restaurant in Fremont." was my first response since this Tom guy was either with the FBI that was following me or he was with John. Either way, I had to figure out which one it was. I was hoping that he worked for John and was sent to help me get this crap straightened out, or get me out of this mess so I could keep my plans to leave with Rose in June.

His response was meant to mess with me, at least that is how I took it as. He said "Well if you don't know what John I would be here to see you about, then I guess I should just leave. I will take it that you have everything in order." Tom stood up, took another sip of the coffee, and started to walk towards the door. I was about to let him go, and I was going to get dressed. Then I got a sinking feeling in my stomach, so I stopped him from walking out the door. I asked Tom to finish his coffee as I went to get dressed. The bastard won this game of chicken.

It did not take me long to get dressed and back out to Tom. I also had a sawed-off shotgun in hand. When I stepped out where Tom was sitting at the kitchen island, I sat the shotgun on the counter. I got myself another cup of coffee. Tom smiled at me and asked if I would pull the trigger if he did anything. I did not know at that time if I would or not. Tom turned it for the barrels to face him. I don't know what he was trying to do, but I took it he was not worried about me shooting him.

Now that he was showing that he was not worried about my gun, we started to talk again. The first thing he said was that I did not have to worry about being followed around anymore. Of course, I wanted to know what he did or what he knew. So I asked as quickly as I could "Why, what is going on and what do you know about me?" I think I was even huffing when I asked him.

Tom must not have been someone who showed his cards unless it would be in his best interest. He told me not to worry about what he knows, but as for being followed, it was his guys following me. Tom said Mick and the others have been seeing people from the government. It did not make me feel better, but it was good to know I was not being followed. I don't know if he meant to say things to bring up more question as a way to screw with me, but he sat there calmly.

"Tom, why have you been following me and what are you here to do?" Tom smiled again when I asked him that. I felt even worse when he said; "Scott, I am here because John's boss has concerns about you. John spoke highly of you. He must of or another guy would have come to see you. I am here to assess what to do. I have three options to choose for you. What I choose will be what you do." He did not change any facial expression, looked me in the eye and said: "One option I have is to have you completely removed."

Well crap, I now understood that Tom was not another lackey like Ferris. Instead, he was with a company that fixes problems, John's boss who I just learned existed, had sent him. John had no way to help me with this and I was in deeper than I had realized. The only thing I guessed was I knew enough about John to be concerned if I was arrested. This was why Tom was in my place drinking my coffee letting me know he could choose if I get killed.

All I could say was "Hell" and Tom said, "That is nicer than most people put it."

We talked about what he had learned and what options he was leaning towards. Option one he could kill me and be done with the job. I personally was not in favor of that option. The second option he said he might tell me later. The good and bad was he was not willing to allow me to be arrested. He told me the third option was to make me disappear as I was planning to do. When I told him about what I was doing with the new identity, he seemed to be on board with what I had already set up. The only thing I was not expecting was the timeline he gave me. He said that I had three weeks to be ready. Since he was being so enjoyable at that point, he told me what would happen if I was not ready. He personally would throw my dead naked and bleached body on the side of some road. I could see that we were going to be such good friends.

Finally, Tom went to leave. Before walking out the door, he said that he did not want anyone to know he was even in the state of Ohio. He also told me to wrap my chest with an ace bandage to help the fractured rib. I was not going to try and find out why, but I would listen to him and not say anything about him or our conversation. Between being scared of him killing me and how Rose would act, telling anyone was the last thing I would do.

Knowing I was not being followed by the FBI or anyone, I

called Mick and Duke to see if they would come over. Mick said he would be able to in the afternoon when he was done with getting some guys set up. Duke, on the other hand, was as free with his time as I was, so he came right over. I asked Duke if he would stop to pick up an ace bandage for my chest.

While I waited, I started to make a list of what I needed from each of them. If I was thinking right, I could get everything done in two weeks. That would give me a week to enjoy with everyone before I left. I wrote on the list for Mick, party in a week. The rest of the list had things on it to help me put everything in order.

I wanted to tell Duke and Mick what I wanted them to do if something happened to me. I was not going to tell them that I had a visitor, but I would figure out what to tell them when they got to my place. I figured I had some time, but Duke did not give me that. He was knocking on my door before I realized it. When he came in, he handed me a brown bag that had a breakfast sandwich in it. He told me that his dad was making some food and gave him two sandwiches in the bag. I looked in the bag, but there was only one sandwich. Duke said he got hungry and with a click of his tongue, he gave me a thumbs up.

After thanking him, I started eating while Duke asked why I wanted him to come over. I never understood why people always ask someone questions when they are eating. Maybe they did not think anything of it because they had not been taught it's rude to talk with food in your mouth. Either way, I held a finger up to say one minute. I was not going to rush eating his dad's sandwich. The one thing about Duke's dad's food, he had some sauce that he made of his own creation and it was unforgettable. I would have always joked with his dad that I would give him ten grand for the recipe. He never accepted my offer or I would have shown up with the money and had to explain where the money came from.

With a swallow and a sip of my coffee, I told Duke that I have some bad feelings. He looked at me and said "Why? What is going on?" I quickly responded. "I have been thinking that John or the group in Detroit would not want me to stay breathing if I get arrested." He thought I was being dramatic. I told him to think about what happened with the deal Mick and I did with the guys in Detroit. Duke started to nod when I also reminded him that Deatz died in a car accident while drinking. I forgot that Duke did not know Deatz other than a meeting or two when I had to stop. I informed Duke that Deatz did not drink or do any more than smoke weed. I could see the look on Duke's face that he fully understood why I was concerned.

We discussed how I needed to update my "Just in case" packages and I asked if there was any cash he was holding for me. He said that he had about fifteen grand of my cash sitting in his room. First thing I had to ask is how long he used his bedroom as his hiding place for things that I had given him. He always told me that no one will find what I gave him. I almost expected him to follow up with saying it is the stuffing in his pillow. Instead of asking any details in fear what I would hear. I only told him that I needed him to bring me what he had.

For some reason, Duke turned on the radio and played with the dial until he found a radio station he liked. He stopped when he heard a song and said how he likes the song. I had to listen closer to remember what it was. The song was Past the Point of Rescue, I believed it was by Hal Kechum. It was a while since I heard the song, but when I remembered the name of the song, I felt sad. All I could think was how I was "Past the Point of Rescue" and no one will ever know what had happened to me. I had to wipe a tear from my face. I was glad that Duke was still looking away from me.

Duke turned around and asked if I was going to run. Before I answered him, he said: "Oh Christ Scott, what the hell?" Then he walked out the door pulling out a cigarette and I followed him. Lighting up a cigarette myself and walking out the door, I said: "It's been years since you called me Scott." It slipped my mind that Duke knew the original plan that had me leaving town. The plan had me going to New York so John could set me up with a new life. This did not leave me much choice but to let Duke in on what I was planning.

"When I disappear, I want you and Mick to go to my lawyer. You will provide him my black book and Mick will provide information about the group in Detroit." I took a hit of my cigarette and exhaled before I continued talking. "I will let my lawyer know that you two will be coming. He will make a deal for you two to turn yourselves in and provide information. I will be going in a few weeks, but I have to figure out how to make sure I am not followed." Duke agreed and said that he had some ideas to make people think I was dead. He wanted to think about it before telling me what he thought I should do.

I was not going to hold my breath for some suggestion. I decided that I had to give Duke my black book. When I began to walk down the stairs, I waved for Duke to follow me. He did and we talked about stupid things till I got in my truck and got my book from the center console. I opened it up and ripped out the page with John's information and the police chief in Fremont. Since the police chief did give me a heads up, I wanted to return the favor and keep him out of it as well. I handed Duke the book and told him to put it in his car. That was the first time that the book was given to someone else. While Duke walked to his car, he opened up the book and said "Are these the amounts you gave these guys? Wow."

I told him that he would be smart not to let anyone know that he had that and he never heard John's name. Considering who was listed in there and the note, someone might get some ideas to get rid of it and whoever had it. That was enough information for him and he put it in his glove box. While Duke was getting back out of his car, he grabbed another bag. This bag had the pharmacy logo on it. He throws the bag to me and it hit the ground. Of course, I was not going to jump or move quickly to get it. It flew past me and Duke started to laugh. While laughing, he said, "Oh yeah, I guess I should have handed it to you." I don't know why he found it funny, but he did.

The day moved fast as I was moving slow. It was not long after Duke took off that Mick showed up. I got myself some lunch and started reading a book. I must have dozed off. I heard Mick stomping up the stairs, then some knocking on my door. As I started to get up, the door started to open and Mick started to yell "Hello, Bearman. Hello, you here?" He must have seen me and came in. He told me to stay seated and went for a glass of water. When he sat down with me, we got into discussing everything. Finally, I told him that he should never say John's name again and he does not know anyone by that name.

It was a similar conversation with Mick asking why I wanted to see him and me saying that I had some bad feelings. Mick asked if he needed to worry and I explained to him what I told Duke they would do if anything happened. He asked what good will that do him. We talked about how important what he knows about all the guns that the people in Detroit purchased from us. He also knew about how they got those gangs in Toledo to fall in line and work with us.

Once he understood the power he had with his knowledge and how to use it, he agreed that he would go to the lawyer with Duke. I got to what it was that I needed from him. I first told him that he should give me twenty thousand dollars and no counterfeit money. He asked why and I told him that I would be signing over the property to him in about a week. He got excited and agreed to have the money in a couple of days. He also told me he stopped printing money since his new guy did not do a good job. I knew John was not happy with the last batch and told me not to send any more till it got back on track. I had told Mick this, but I figured he would try to improve it. It looked as if I was wrong, but I could not take it personally.

I had to let Mick take the business where he wanted. Another reason I was not going to let it bother me was that I knew it all would be gone in less than a month. What I found funny was Mick still wanted advice from me. In fact, he asked for some advice while we were talking about one of the guys that worked for Mark. The guy was now working with us but was trying to get more area for himself. The problem was, Mick started acting like a supplier and not like a boss to those guys.

I told Mick he should have a party to celebrate the house being in his name. While he has all his guys together, find out if they would prefer to work for us or only have us supply them. I reminded Mick that if they choose to be on their own, it would be like Toledo. We only supply drugs, but they could go elsewhere and there is nothing we could do about it. Mick said he liked that and wanted to take the risk. We discussed what would be involved with both options. The whole time, I was asking myself why I am going through the effort to plan and explain. I guess I still had a little hope that things would turn around for me.

After about two more hours of talking, I told Mick that I was going to make a few phone calls. I had to get things in order for him to have the house. While getting up, Mick said he will put his money together and bring it over. For what we did, having a lot of cash lying around was a common benefit. Mick asked for a sandwich. While he was making it, he mentioned that he has not seen anyone following him for a few days. As he took a bite and chewed the sandwich, he asked if that means we are in the clear. First I told him to finish chewing before talking and explain how I don't want to see his food as he chews. He took another bite and gave me a sharp look while he chewed.

This was something I was not sure how to answer. There was a lot to worry about. It could be any time that someone came and arrested us. If I got lucky, I could carry out my plan and everyone would get out safe. So I told Mick that we were good at that time. With a halfhearted smile, he walked out and I was alone again. I figured Mick did not fully believe me. That did not matter, the only thing I worried about was how much time I had.

I went back to my kitchen and pulled off the side kickboard on the island. Reaching into the black hole, I hoped that nothing would move. The thought gave me a little smile. That was it, I found what I was trying to get. A screw sticking out of a long wooden box I made to hide things. The box was about three-quarters of the length of the island. When I first slid it under there, I only had a pound of weed and about two thousand dollars.

This time, when I pulled it out, there was a lot more. I put had put money in the box every week with about fifty percent of every dollar I made. There was close to three hundred thousand in the box. You would think that much money would be a large pile and very impressive. In fact, there were about twenty–nine bundles of hundred dollars bills and a few stacks of smaller bills. I put it all into a duffel bag and the money did not cover the bottom of the bag. I filled it with clothes and a gun so I was ready to go and had nothing to worry about. I knew Rose never got into my side of the closet so I put the duffle on the floor and covered it with some clothes and rags.

The final few hours I had to myself before Rose got home was spent trying to wrap my chest so it was not too tight or too loose. Either way, it was not very much fun to do. We can say that someone with my kind of humor watching me would have gotten a good laugh. I did not get a laugh from it though.

Chapter Sixteen

It had been a few days and it was also the day for me to get my tattoo along with some other things. Being my first tattoo, I was nervous about it but happy to have the scar on my back covered up. I knew that it would be easier to have people see a tattoo instead of a scar. It would be one less lie I would have to worry about. There would be enough to have to remember and not let it slip. I had to start preparing for the end of Scott Bearman. As far as the world as a whole would know, in a week or two, Scott Bearman would have vanished. I was even thinking of having Duke spread a rumor that I had pissed off some guys in Detroit. Since Mick was going to turn over what he knew about them, it would seem realistic.

While I was putting on my shirt and making sure it was loose enough not to rub, Rose yelled to get my attention. Since we did not have a big place, it did not take much to get each other's attention. When I walked out, she was in the kitchen fixing herself some lunch. She was trying to be smart when she said "You better eat too, it's not good to get a tattoo on an empty stomach. Why do you think I am making the sandwich and fries." I caught what she said, but I was not going to act surprised that she decided to get one too.

"So what are you going to get? A pretty little ladybug, a tribal, or maybe a unicorn? Just tell me you're not getting a tramp stamp." From the look on Rose's face, the tramp stamp comment had her upset. She walked into the bedroom mumbling what I thought was "I can't believe you would think I would get a tramp stamp." Either way, she was in there for a few minutes.

When she came out, she was wearing her swimsuit top. She looked very sexy in it with the small little strings tied behind her neck and mid-back. If it was not for the appointment at the tattoo shop, we would have not made it out the door. That was till she put one of my old tee shirts that looked like a short dress hiding a pair of Jean shorts. She must not have had anything on her mind like I did, because she handed me my keys and said: "Let's go."

As we went down the road, I could easily tell that she was still bothered by the tramp stamp comment. I did everything I could to make her feel better and have the trip be a memory that we both could look back on. When we got a few miles outside of Fremont, she said: "You know what you are?" Then she gave me a smile that I took as forgiveness. After that, it was a good trip with us talking about what to expect. Rose even joked about how she wanted to bet that I would cry or whimper. We made these kinds of bets, but we never bet money. It was always open-ended. The winner could claim whatever at any given time.

This time, I parked in the alley behind the shop. I found it odd that Jerry's bike was there. It was years since I last saw him and from what I heard, he only came in for special clients and to handle business issues. I was hoping that Ryan would hear me knock and open the door. Instead, when we got out of the truck, Jerry opened the door and told us to come in, almost like he was waiting for us.

Once we were inside, Ryan came out of his room. There were three rooms for the guys to work and Jerry had himself set up in the front. It was an open area with a curtain if he needed to do some work that the client didn't want anyone to see. Other than that, the curtain was open while he was there. He had me lay down on my side and still moving slowly, Jerry asked what happened to me. I explained the whole thing with Cameron and how I had a fractured rib. He was upset about it, but just said he was sorry to hear that and would be as easy going as he could.

We talked while he was making the final adjustments to the drawing. Once he had it the way that we both were happy with it, I took off my shirt. He put the drawing of the Celtic cross on my back shoulder to cover up the scar. Jerry said that he was not going to ask about the scar and I said thanks. When I got in a comfortable position, I looked up to see a full-length mirror straight in front of me. I could not help myself and started to laugh. I laugh so much that I hurt doing it, but if you saw what I did, you would laugh too.

Jerry was confused and told me that this was a new one for him and asked why I was laughing. I pointed to the mirror and pulled myself together to explain. I asked him if he ever watched prison movies. He nodded and I said, "In the movies, there is always a big guy covered in tattoos that come up to the new guy. The tattoo guy makes him his new bitch." That is when he started to laugh and said, "If we were in prison, you would be my new bitch."

He then said jokingly that I shared a crib with his daughter, so he wouldn't do that to me. I thanked him for that and he told me to hold still. I did as he said, even when he would adjust me to get a better angle. When he moved me, I felt the discomfort of it. We were about twenty-five minutes in when he told me that he had finished up the line work and the easy part was coloring in the drawing.

As he got up to stretch and get a drink, I joked that he shouldn't make it too strong. He smiled and told me it's only water. When he walked away Rose and Ryan walked in to see the progress. They seemed impressed and I was too, when Ryan held up a mirror so I could see it off the full-length mirror. I asked Rose to come in front of me so I could see hers.

It was good if I had to say so myself. She got a single red rose lying on a strip of grass. It looked as if the grass went back further to give depth. She was happy when I told her how good it looked and Ryan said thank you before she did. He also said that we could just include her tattoo in what he quoted me. That made Rose happy to get a free tattoo and a nice looking one at that.

I reached in my pocket and got him the keys to my truck and said I forgot the money in the center console. He smiled and took my keys. When he returned, he said that he left the care instructions in my truck. "Everything I needed is in the center console." With a thank you, Ryan was off to do his own thing. It was not long that Jerry came back and said he was ready to do some coloring. As I felt the machine he used to tattoo me, I looked at the mirror. Now there was not just a big tattooed guy behind me, but a small petite girl looking over his shoulder. It was a sight to see.

When Jerry finished up and we looked at the final work, I was very happy. A Celtic cross with my family's birthstones in it would be my reminder of my family where ever I went. Jerry asked Rose to get some Aquaphor from Ryan. When she left, he told me that the paperwork Ryan gave me can be taken to get my new driver's license. I asked how he knew what Ryan did for me. He said that he was teaching him. I never knew that Jerry ran that kind of business as I thought I knew most of the criminals in my area.

After all our thank you and chitchat, we were about to leave. When I asked what I owed Jerry he said "I saw what Cameron did to you growing up and I did nothing. I don't know if it would have made a difference if I did, but that always bothered me. Consider this tattoo my apologies and best of luck." I gave him a big handshake and as I pulled my hand back, he told me to take care of myself. With that, we were out the door and on our way home.

Rose asked if we could stop by her mom's house to show off her new tattoo. I agreed, but I was not looking forward to it. Her mom hated me and at times told Rose that she should do better. Her mom treated me with a polite attitude when I was there. Even that time, when we pulled up to the old red house with a white porch, her family came out to greet us.

While we sat on the porch talking, Rose and her sister went out to the barn to see the new litter of kittens. I tried not to be left alone with her mom, but there was nothing I could do, it was just her mom and me on that porch. To my surprise, I heard "You know I am not your biggest fan. I have nothing against you personally, but my daughter deserves better. However, I am sorry to hear what happened to you. I know you had it rough with what Cameron put you through. You understand that I don't want Rose to have to worry about someone like Cameron knocking on her door?"

Rose's mom waited for me to answer her. I almost thought that she was planning on me to get upset and make a big show of it. Instead, I told her that I agreed with her. I explained that I knew that Rose could do better and I try to be better for her. Her mom's mouth hung open while I talked. After a few minutes of talking, the last thing her mom said to me before Rose and her sister came back was "You are a better man than I figured. Thank you."

When Rose came back, she was saying how she wanted one of the kittens when it gets old enough. It was cute to see her that way. I told her ok and she and her family went back to talking. With them distracted, I took a walk out to the cow pasture. There was a tree in the middle of the pasture that I liked to sit under. I sat there looking at the light coming through the leaves. It was a nice view, but I knew it was coming to an end. Seeing a few leaves changing colors reminded me of that. The seasons where about to change as well.

I must have sat there for half an hour when I heard Rose calling me. During my walk back up to the house, a cow came up to me. It walked right next to me all the way to the fence. Once I went through the gate, it turned and walked to the other cows.

That seemed strange to me, but it was something that I thought would stay with me. As if it was saying goodbye or something. I could have also over thought it and made it more than it was. Cows never seemed to be the smartest of animals to me, but they are the tastiest.

We spent the rest of the day at our place. I ran into some of the friends we were going to meet up with that day Cameron kicked my ass when Rose and I was walking. They showed up about two hours after we got home and had a pizza with them. While the girls talked and had a good time, I poured myself a glass of bourbon and grabbed a book. Then I went outside to be by myself. I did not read a lot; I mostly sat there with my drink and watched the sky. I felt a little chill in the air, but nothing to make me get a flannel.

Rose popped her head out the door and gave me a slice of the pizza. She told me that Duke was bringing Jenny over, so I would have him to talk to while our place was filled with her friends. I don't know if she called Jenny or if Jenny called us, but it was still good either way. Duke and I could always talk, even if it was about the most pointless stuff that no one would care to hear about.

Everyone left after a few hours. When the last person pulled out, Rose told me about what they talked about. She could not believe what her friend Sheri said. I did not know which one was

Sheri, and Rose did not care or pay any attention if I knew. She told me how Sheri said how she felt that I deserved what Cameron did. I took it that Sheri was not trying to stay friends with Rose. There had to be something, but that was not something I would touch. After Rose got done talking, she asked what Duke and I talked about. I laughed and said we talked about shit.

She looked upset that I did not tell her. That was till I clarified that we talked about some concerns and before I got into more details, she stopped me. I don't blame her, it was a conversation that only a couple young guys would have. Duke and I did talk about my tattoo and about how two lower-level guys had gotten arrested. This got me thinking that things are moving forward. It was not something I wanted Rose to worry about it. The protection was done and my guys where back on their own.

After a good night of sleep, we woke up early and got things going. Rose got ready for school and I called my lawyer. After hanging up, Rose wanted to know why I was calling Harold who was my lawyer. I explained that Mick was buying the house and I was cleaning out anything that could hold us in Ohio. She smiled and kissed me and walked out the door. When the door closed, I wrapped my ribs and finished getting around. I was getting good at wrapping my ribs and I was getting used to the pain to where it did not bother me as bad.

Being wrapped, dressed, and hungry, I decided to make a

fried egg sandwich. Nothing starts the day like a good breakfast. I put two greasy eggs topped with lettuce, baloney, mayonnaise, and cheese shoved between two pieces of bread. I took a few bits when my phone rang. It turned out to be my lawyer returning my call. Harold did not give me a chance to say hello. I think he was talking the moment I picked up the phone. He was mid-sentence when I put the phone to my ear.

"...and I have your paperwork ready. If you would like to come by around one o'clock, we can get it finalized." Harold took a breath and I got to respond. "Harold, Good morning. First I need to know what all you want me to bring and how much do I owe you? Secondly, I need to discuss something with you that needs to be private." Harold started talking again and said, "you're not going to tell me you're a democrat are you?" With a laugh, I said no and we discussed what was needed from Mick and me. He made a few jokes and hung up without a word. That gave me a few hours to get Mick and drive to Bowling Green.

I got lucky when I called the new phone number Mick had given me. He had recently had a phone line installed at the house. I started to think that Mick would live in that house for the rest of his life. He was trying to make it his house from the day he moved in, even though he said he was only there for a few months. I kind of knew that was not going to be the case, now it would be his.

I told him about our meeting with my lawyer and gave him all the details. I could hear the excitement in his voice. He hung up the phone and I lay down on the couch. I put in a movie called the Quick and the Dead. I did not get too far into the movie when Mick showed up. I swear that boy had wings on his car. He knocked on the door as he walked into my place. I looked up at him and jokingly asked if he was in a hurry to stop being a squatter. He did not like it too much or that is how I took it when he flipped me off. Either way, there was time before we had to worry about going.

In that time, we talked about the business and what options he was looking at when the bottom drops out. He had to make plans for when everything we were doing came to an end. He told me that he thought it would be funny if he went into the FBI. He laughed till I said that I believed that they only accept people with college degrees. As he got a serious look on his face, he followed up with, "I will figure it out. I have enough money to get me by for a while. How about you?"

I shook my head and told him that I would not have to worry about that for some time. Mick got a serious look again when I reminded him that either one of two things was going to happen. He was remembering that I would be going to prison or dead. After explaining to him why I was having him turn over his information, he lowered his head. He said he understood. I could tell he was bothered by what I had to face. He kept asking how I was dealing with it and if there was any other way. He also asked what he should say if he was asked about Jay Himlee. I quickly replied to him with an angry voice; "You never say anything about that night. As far as anyone needs to know, you only know that Jay was an ass and a trouble maker. They will not let you off for what we did to him." Before I said anything more, he stopped me.

I took a few breathes to calm myself when Mick told me that he did not know I was wanted. He apologized to me and I looked up to the wall clock. It was noon and I told Mick that we had to go. He jumped up with a relaxed face, asking if we could ride together, but I told him that we could not this time. We both got into our vehicles and Mick followed me to my Lawyer. It wasn't long after we arrived that we were put into a conference room. I could see that Mick was not used to being in a nice office. He kept looking around like he had never has seen such wonders.

Harold walked in with two other guys. One guy sat next to Mick and introduced himself. Harold sat at the head of the table and the other guy sat next to me. According to Harold, these guys were acting as our agents of interest or something like that. They were to make sure that we had legal counsel to make sure we did not screw over each other. Harold laid down a stack of papers and asked Mick if he had the money. Mick put a bag of cash on the table.

Harold gave Mick a what– the– hell kind of look and asked if he knew that a check would have been a better option. Harold did not wait for Mick to say anything and asked if I wanted everyone to wait until I counted the money. I looked at Mick and told Harold that I was not worried about it. With that out of the way, we started to sign the paperwork. During the entire time, the other two guys did not say a word. Once everything got signed, the two other guys got up and left and still did not say anything. Mick had a smile when he was told that he had become an official homeowner.

Mick gave me a big hug and thanked me. The three of us talked for a short time. It was time for me to talk to Harold alone and get a few final issues addressed. I told Mick that I would see him at his house warming party and to remember what we discussed. With that, Mick walked out the door at a nice fast pace. I imagine he wanted to share his news with someone. I thought he had started to go on some dates with a girl, but he would never say.

Harold asked me what I else he could do as soon as the door clicked shut. I held my hand out towards the chair and we both sat back at the conference table. This time we were next to each so we did not have to talk loudly. Harold reminded me that he charges by the hour. I got to the point and told him that shortly, I would be vanishing. I let him know that people would think I am dead at that point.

He said that sounds like something he could not help me with. I said "You will be helping my buddy Duke and that Mick guy that just left. I also want you to destroy any files you have other than our retainer agreement. I need you to handle those guys with negotiating a deal with whomever it would be that could keep them out of trouble. They will be providing information on me and where I got my money." Before I could continue, Harold asked: "Do I want to know all the details about how you got your money?" My only response was "When I am gone, it won't matter. You will have your money and I am giving you a nice advance payment, too."

Reaching into the bag of money Mick just gave me to buy the house, I pulled out a stack of cash, counted out five thousand dollars and slid it over to him. When he slid it closer to him, I said I need a receipt for that. While he walked into his office to get me a receipt that I paid him, I went to my truck. When I came back, I had a box about the size of a shoebox. When I got back in Harold's lobby, he was sitting in one of the chairs waiting for me. We exchanged what we both held. I had asked him to contact everyone that has a letter in the box if Duke or Mick show up.

Harold told me that he was not happy about this as it sounded bad, but he was my paid lawyer. He stopped me by his front doors and said the last thing he ever would. "I will destroy all the documents that could have anything that could be used against you. My people are finishing the paperwork for the house on our end. I will send a copy to the buyer and a copy to your address we have on file. You take care and I will always be here if you need a lawyer." I gave him a smile and a thank you, and then I was out the door and on my way.

I did not know where I was off to. Not at first at least. When I got to route six and twenty-three, I decided that I would go to my mom and Paul's house and get a bottle of homemade wine. Paul had retired but worked part time to keep himself busy. He told me a few times that any man that does not do anything all day, every day is a waste of space. So it was a toss-up if he would be at his job or working at home.

When I pulled into the drive, I saw his truck parked in front of the garage. I was glad to see he was home. As I parked my truck off to the side of the garage, I saw Paul walking out of the back barn. He walked up towards me, so I started to head his way. The first thing he said was that he was glad I was there; he needed a hand fixing a piece of equipment for his job.

Paul knew that I was not the most mechanical person, but I could turn a wrench. After some instructions and him pointing out what I needed to do I followed his lead. We both began doing what was needed. I had my hand up in the motor. Paul told me that some people showing a badge came in asking the officers in town if they knew me. They had a few other questions, but Paul said they went into a different room to discuss it. I think he was waiting until I could not go anywhere to bring that up.

We talked and I did not hide anything from him. Even though I was not mechanical, I enjoyed talking while fixing something. Doing some hard work helps clear the mind. By the time we finished, the motor was running nicely. Paul said that they thought that it was past repairs, but we showed them. He laughed about that and patted me on the back. It was not long after that, we cleaned up and I realized my shirt was covered in grease.

I did not say it, but I was thinking that would be one less shirt to fit in my bag. Paul asked why I was stopping by other than ruining a good shirt. I smiled and asked what other reason would I have. He did not skip a beat and started listing all the things people my age would be there for. I told him he forgot the wine and I pulled a bottle from a box I was standing next to.

He pulled out another and told me to take both, and then we walked to the house. While we were there, I grabbed a tee shirt from him. He handed me a gold ring with a diamond set in the middle of a square top and a black background for the diamond. I thought about how nice and simple the ring was. I went to hand it back to him and he said: "you know I don't wear rings other than my wedding ring. With the type of work I do, other rings would be destroyed. This ring was my fathers. I want you to have it in case something happens, you'll already have it."

The ring might of not have been the most expensive ring around, but I promised to always wear it. To me, that ring had a higher value than anything I owned. We talked for another twenty minutes before I headed home. During my drive, I could only think about how my family would take the news that I was dead or missing. There was no good option to get out of the mess I got myself into. I could only hope that they did not take it too hard. I also think Paul was expecting me to disappear.

When I got back to my place, Rose was home. She welcomed me with telling me she got us some sandwiches from the bar in Gibsonburg. They were always good about letting teenagers in for food. There was not a lot of selection in the small towns.

When I picked up my sandwich, Rose noticed my new ring. She did not hesitate to ask me about it. I honestly believed that she was worried some girl gave it to me. That was something I did not want to have her dwell on. As I have said before, I would rather be shot at again before having her get completely angry.

So I explained about it being a gift from Paul and how it had been passed to him from his father. I did not realize it at first, but I was smiling looking at the ring when I told her. She came and gave me a nice hug, then took the ring to look at it. After that, it was a typical night. It was a typical next few days until the day of Mick's party.

Chapter Seventeen

Mick's party was good. It was not only a group of drug dealers, but everyone Mick knew and their girlfriends. It reminded me of the barn party where I asked Rose to marry me. I even had Rose come with me. It was her first time at the house and it was not even mine anymore. Rose saw a few girls that she knew. As for the people who knew me, it was not a complete group of people with open arms. They saw me as a villain. The kind you see on TV where they only want to destroy everything and cause trouble.

What I found funny was, they were at a party for the guy who had taken over my business. Mick did not have the same reputation as I did. He was known in our world, but outside of that, I guess I was still the face.

About an hour in, I saw Mick waving me to come into the house. I went in, but Rose stayed out to talk to a new friend she was making. As I was walking towards the house, I stop to say hi to Tony, the same guy who helped me in the fight with Jay

Himlee's guys. He introduced his new girlfriend to me and asked about Rose and Jenny. I pointed out Rose while asking if he could keep an eye out for her. I did not want some drunk idiot to get the wrong idea. Tony being the good guy he was, asked his girlfriend if she would like to meet Rose and maybe hang out. That is what they did too. Later, Rose told me that she hit it off with Tony's girlfriend and the four of us were to have dinner. I was happy to do it too, if we could.

When I got in the house, I saw our guys sitting around. They all stood up when I walked in. Those dumb asses knew I was not really in charge anymore, but more of a helping hand for Mick. I joked about how special I must be to have so many dicks get up for me. We laughed and joked around a bit. When Mick came back in the room, he asked the guys and me to go into the back room. It no longer looked close to what I had. Mick even got rid of my hiding shelf behind the picture and he took down the painting.

The group of us sat down in what had become a kind of bedroom with a futon, chair, and a small TV. I would not have told Mick, but it made me sad to see the room that I sat with a mob boss become a high school boys room. As we all were looking around, Mick asked how everyone liked what he had done with the house. Most of the guys were young, so it would have been the same thing they would have done. They all told him so, but before I said anything, he asked if I would like to start the meeting.

I did not hesitate and said "You guys know I am backing away from everything here. Mick is the top guy now. We have been discussing the future of what we have built here. Mick feels that you guys should have a voice before the final decision is made." I was interrupted by a guy named Greg asking why I was leaving and why did he not know about this. Come to find out, none of the guys knew I was getting out. Mick had not told them anything, so they all kept going as though I was calling the shots. They also kept reminding people what happens to those that owe me money.

I wanted to say something to Mick right there, but it wasn't worth it. I instead told the guys everything and why I was done. I don't know why, but Greg seemed to be the most bothered by this. He got up and went to grab me, but one of the other guys stopped him. Finally I got tired of these guys overreacting, so I stood up as fast as I could. It was not that fast with the rib and all. I said "You guys need to let me finish or I will not even bother. I will go back out with Rose and enjoy the party. This could be the last time I am here with you all."

That got them to shut up. Greg said he was sorry and everyone else asked me to say what I needed to. I told them how we were losing our protection with the police and there are feds or someone coming after us. They looked worried and I knew they should be. I finally got to the point and told them that Mick would like to cut everything back. He was planning to only supply the drugs until everything settled down. Then Kyle stood up and asked if that means they were on their own.

Kyle said "Bearman, you know I am here to back whatever you think is best. Are you say that we are back to when you started this? Are we no longer helping each other?" He sat down and everyone looked at me, waiting for my answer. I did not understand why Mick did not answer any of these guys, but I would not leave them on their own. After a moment of thinking about it, I decided I would do something. Something that would allow these guys to keep what I built alive. So I answered Kyle with "You guys are already doing the work and at this point, you don't need us. I don't want to offer you an option, I want you to do what you are doing now. You call each other and work together to maintain what you got. Protect each other and back each other up when it's needed. Mick will be your supplier, but you guys no longer give up your cash. As long as you guys stay working together, Mick will give you a discount. Anyone else would pay more. You guys are now the company."

Mick got a smile on his face because this gave him what he wanted. The other guys at that point were no longer taking orders, but they had a real say in what would happen. I could hear the excitement they had built up as they talked. As they no longer were looking to me for answers, I got up and walked out and back to Rose. When I got out there, Rose and Tony's new girlfriend were still talking. When Tony saw me, he yelled at me. I could not make out what he was saying until I got closer. When I heard him, he was saying "They forgot that I am here." I gave a little smile and a nod. When Rose looked away, she shook her cup to let me know it was empty. Being who I was, I grabbed her cup and kissed her before I turned around to fill her cup. Tony walked with me to talk and get his girlfriend a drink too.

On our way to the keg Tony asked, "What is going on? You walked in the house looking stressed, but now you look as if a weight has been lifted." Tony smiled and filed the cups. When he handed me my beer I asked him how much he knows about what I did. Tony drank a few beers, kept smiling and a small fire off to the side of us showed his red face. I figured he would not remember a whole lot I said, so I told him. I explained how I believed that I had saved what I built and knowing it would go on made me happy. To my surprise, Tony said "So you are finally done. I understand now. Hopefully, you can find a good life now and real happiness."

The rest of the night was filled with nothing more than the four of us talking. I did not think once about Mick changing everything I built. I could not believe he kept telling people I was still running things. I only could let that go and move on. Nothing had me bothered about anything, at least not till the following morning. The morning after the party, Rose was sleeping in and was dead to the world. She drank plenty and an earthquake would not wake her up. I had a bit of a hangover, but my real headache came from the person knocking on my door. My first thought was who knocks on someone's door the morning after a party.

When I answered the door, Tom Stone stood there sipping on some green drink. It was not like my stomach was very strong at that time. Tom's drink did not look tasty, but he seemed to like it. I turned around, left the door open, and went to my refrigerator. I found pizza from a day or two before. As I started to eat it, Tom asked if I was able to talk. I did not want to temp fate and have Rose overhear the conversation.

We went out on the landing and closed the door behind me. I knew it could not be good news with him already there. He did not give me time to say anything. It seemed that it was becoming a trend with people. Tom told me that he had made his decision and I could come with him or be found dead. That did not seem like much of a choice to me, but I was going to leave anyway. So, I choose to go with him, considering I did not have an urge to learn what a small pine box was like on the inside.

When I asked how much time I had until we left, Tom said I had till the middle of the week. I naturally tried to get more time, but I did not have a valid answer when he asked why I needed more time. He told me the two reasons that he felt he was giving me enough time. The first one was he knew I had spent my time saying goodbye to everyone without saying it. The second was that his contact told him that a raid was scheduled on Thursday.

I thought for a moment when I told him that Wednesday night would work for me. He told me that he had a plan. If I did what he said people would think I was dead. All I needed to do was take another guy to the Risingsun Park. Tom walked down the steps after that and about three steps down, he said that it would be best to bring a guy I didn't care about. With that said, he was gone and I no longer was sure if my headache was from drinking or Tom. I believed it was more from Tom.

I went through my memories of who I could use for whatever Tom had planned. The worst thing was, I had figured that Tom would kill the guy. Then I remembered James. He owed me and I never collected from him. From what I remembered of him, he always owed us money. Since I did not see Mick going to collect, I guessed I would.

Before I started making calls to find him, I went into the bedroom to see if Rose had shown any signs of waking up, but she was not even close to waking up. She must have drank more than I realized. Most likely she would hate the world when she woke up, but until then, I had calls to make.

It took me about twenty minutes until someone knew where James was. The person I got a hold of said he would be going to meet up with him shortly and would have him call me. With a thank you and I owe you one, I was done. Next, I called Duke but could not find him so I called Mick.

Mick did answer and once he knew it was me calling, he told me some bad news. He said that two of the guys who we had as our "area managers" got arrested after the party. Greg was one of them and he called Mick for help. Mick only knew my lawyer and called him. We talked more about it and Mick was scared. I knew if he got arrested, he would not do himself any favors. As for Duke, I was not sure and did not want to tempt it.

I told Mick that he will find Duke first and then make plans to be at Harold's office as early as possible on Monday. Mick was not happy to hear that he was ending everything voluntarily. That was untill I reminded him of the other option. He had no urge to spend any time locked up. My final words to Mick was for him to find a hotel for the weekend and bring Duke. I informed him we could not talk again. He tried to say something, but I hung up.

There was no reason to drag it out. The rest of the day, Rose and I spent the day being lazy. I did not want her to think anything was wrong. She was sick with the brown bottle flu and that was one of the times I could say that Rose did not look her best. I joked to myself that I was happy how that would not be the last way I saw her.

Sunday came and Rose was back to her beautiful self and was off with her dad. They were doing a family cookout. I told Rose that I had some business to wrap up and a final deal to get the product. An hour after Rose left, I got a call from a Columbus phone number. The caller id box also had a church name on it. To my shock, it was Duke.

I could not stop myself and asked what was he doing at a church in Columbus. We went back and forth, then he told me he was at his uncle's church on Saturday and back Sunday evening. He told me that Jenny called him Saturday night and said Mick was looking for him. He called Mick and Mick repeated everything I said to him. Duke said he called me the first chance he got to confirm that he needed to go to the lawyers on Monday.

I made sure I was clear as I could be over the phone. It was not easy to have the conversation and knowing it would be our last. As soon as I hung up, my oldest friend would be gone from my life. I considered a lot of things that could happen when I started selling drugs. I never thought of any of the events that happened would lead to changing my name and meeting Mr. Stone. As it had to happen, Duke said he had to run and hung up. That was that and I sat down to think.

The next few days passed very quickly and Wednesday arrived. I kissed Rose goodbye and told her that I had a deal to make later in the evening. She had an upset look on her face and I promised that it would be my last deal, and I was out. She gave me another kiss for the last time and we told each other that we loved one another. After that, she was off to school.

I got my guns and loaded them. I wanted to be ready and hoping not to use the P90 I was still holding onto. I had not gotten to play with it since we first got them from John. I packed another duffel and took everything out to my truck. I remember every step to my truck and every other thing that happened that day. It's hard to forget the end of your life when you know its coming.

With everything ready to go and James saying he would be ready by six in the evening, I decided to write a note for Rose. I figured since I would not be returning home, I did not want her to feel bad or blame herself for anything. The letter was simple since the box I gave Harold had a more in-depth letter. The letter said:

Rose,

I don't have a good feeling about my deal tonight, but I need the money to make sure we are able to have a future. I want you to know that I love you. Considering my odd feeling about tonight and people getting arrested, I am worried something might happen. In case something does happen, you should not hold onto me for too long. Your happiness is important to me. Remember me and the good times we had, remember the times that were only ours, but find the same light you shared with me. I love you and always try to make yourself as happy as you made me.

Scott Bearman

With that written, I folded it and hung it on the refrigerator. There were a few hours to kill, so I went to do some of the things I knew I would miss. I got some Ribs in New Riegel and then sat on the side of an empty country road. It was a few hours before I realized what time it was as I looked at my watch. It was six already and I got on my way as quickly as I could. I had never been late for anything till that day. When I got to James, it was six-thirty and he was standing in Kmart parking lot with someone. I never saw the guy before, nor did I have time to find out anything about the guy. I pulled up next to the car and rolled down my window.

"James, let's go, get in the truck. I am running late and we have business at seven." After I said that, James waved and said something to his friend, then climbed into the passenger seat. He was much more relaxed compared to the first time I told him to get into my truck. If he only knew, he would have been more concerned. Instead, not knowing that I turned over everything, he thought that he was getting to do a drug deal with the boss. He even seemed happy but trying not to show it.

We got on our way, but luckily we only had a fifteen-minute drive. I got off route twenty-three and onto Salem St. to get to the park. I knew the park gates should be closed or about to be closed and locked at the time. I guess I did not think about Tom Stone planning ahead and taking care of things. As James and I got to the gate, Tom opened the gate and into the park we went. As I parked in the first spot I could, Tom closed the gate and locked it. Tom walked up to my side of the truck and got into the back.

"Go down the service road to the end and we can take care of things back there. You made the right choice coming, by the way." I could see James wanting to reply. He was trying to look tough to me, but I shook my head to indicate I did not want him to say anything to Tom's comment. I did reply with asking what service road. In all the years living in and around Risingsun, I never knew that the walking path was partly a service path for the village. I noticed it for the first time when Tom pointed at the gray large path. That was all it took and I followed his instructions.

Down the path we went. It felt odd to drive down it. I wondered if anyone would call the police to report us for driving down the path. Someone might think it was someone from the village. Either way, it did not matter and it would be over soon enough. I was only hoping that Tom did not lie to me and plan on taking me out. I just could not think why he had me bring someone if he did plan to kill me. I guess I had to wait and see what was planned. Considering I was going somewhere I did not know existed in a town I lived in for years, it all would be interesting.

We got to an open area with a concrete pad that was wrapped around by a bunch of trees. He had a black Ford F-150 short bed quad cab parked there. When we got closer, I saw that it had a tonneau cover on it. It was a good looking truck, but he did not seem like a truck guy. I stopped thinking about it when he told me to park on the other side of the concrete pad. Once I put it in park and turned the truck off, Tom got out. I told James to stay in the truck and I pointed at a double-barrel sawed-off shotgun next to his leg. James gave me a thumbs up and I got out too.

Tom stood between our trucks. When I got up to him, what he said made me even more nervous. He said "I am taking you with me to see my boss for an interview. This is part of your interview, too. We need two dead bodies and you brought one already." Then he turned towards his truck and said: "I brought the other one." I heard the tailgate of his truck bang as he dropped it opened. He reached into the truck bed and pulled out some guy. Dropping the guy to the ground, he told the guy to behave himself.

Tom asked if I was willing to kill someone, then looked back at the guy on the ground. I understood what he was saying. I felt bad for James since I knew he was dead no matter what. As for whoever the other guy was, I was hoping that he deserved what was coming. I waved James to come over to me and he came with the shotgun in hand. I told him to point the gun at the guy on the ground and he did not think twice to do what I said. I guess I got a chance to use the P90 and I went to get it from my back seat.

With the gun in hand, Tom cut the bindings around the guy's feet and picked him up. He walked him to where James already stood and waited for me to join them. When I got to where they all stood, Tom removed a bag over the guy's head. I was happy and surprised at the same time. I looked at the face of Dan with his brown eyes and the scar I gave him. James must have known Dan and been friendly because he seemed upset to see Dan standing there in front of us like he was.

James started to tell me that he would not stand for us to do anything to Dan. He ranted for a short time. That was, till I accepted that the interview could be a death sentence for all of us if I did not pass. I did not let that set in and shot James. He hit the ground and I heard him making groaning sounds as he laid there. I felt even worse and shot him in the head to end it for him. With that shot, James no longer made any sounds. He was completely dead.

It must have been Dan's first time to see a dead body. The

horror on his face showed a reaction I had never seen from him. To see his fear and know that I was the reason for it gave me a rush. I don't know what made me do it, but I reached down and grabbed the shotgun that James had. As I picked it up, I said: "In for a penny, in for a pound." I asked for Tom to remove the restraints holding Dan's hands.

I guessed that Tom wanted to see what would happen. He did as I asked and removed the zip ties holding Dan's hands. As Dan started to rub his wrist, I held out the shotgun for him to take. He looked at the gun and started to plead with me. He said: "Scott, I don't know why you're doing this. What did I do for you to want to kill me? What did James do? If you let me go, I won't say anything."

What he said pissed me off and I shoved the shotgun into his chest. He grabbed it and kept talking while trying to get out of what was coming for him. Finally, I got tired of him talking and I shut him up. My words would run through his head for the very short time he had left. "You won't say anything? Like you said you would stay out of my business and you went to a meeting with Jay Himlee causing me to kill Jay. Like you would not try to cross me after that and then you ran to Ferris. You thought you could work your way in and go around me. The final thing you did was to talk to some cops that were not on my pay. You knew the code others use to see if a cop was with me. Now my life here is over and I am losing everything. I am not going to let you go, I am not going to let you see tomorrow."

Once I finished, Dan pulled up the shotgun and pulled the trigger. I heard Tom yell and try to stop him. I stood there looking at Dan and listen to the gun make a dry fire click. Both Tom and Dan had a confused look on their face. With a smile, I asked if he believed that I would hand him a loaded gun. Then I shot him in the knees. I expected him to scream and curse like the guy I shot in the crotch. I hoped that guy died, but he would not be happy in life if he survived.

Dan would not have the same chance. Instead, I was going to make him suffer and make sure he died painfully. That was till Tom stepped towards me and said we needed to go. This made me upset, as I was not going to leave with Dan alive and I told Tom so. To my surprise, Tom told me to finish Dan off and grab my stuff from my truck. I waited to kill Dan so he could feel the pain a bit longer and I got my bags.

While I was putting my stuff in Tom's truck, I asked what his plan was. He said that he was going to put the dead bodies in my truck with some welding tanks. He pointed at some canisters labeled ethyne that was tied down in the back of his truck bed. Tom was going to light the truck on fire. I learned that day that ethyne is what welders use. Tom taught me that the gas will burn over six thousand degrees when it is mixed with oxygen. He was telling me that fact as he put the tank in the back seat and a yellow balloon around the opening of the tank.

I decided the best way to finish Dan would be one of the ways that I had nightmares about. Tom told me to leave James where he was. I told him that I did not want to waste another bullet on Dan, and Tom pulled out his gun. I stopped him and explained what I wanted to do. After that, we lifted Dan up and put him in the driver seat of the truck. I tossed the keys on the floorboards. Tom handed me a gas can and pointed to my truck. Nothing was needed to be said to know what Tom wanted me to do. I went to the passenger side, opened the door, and poured the gas all over the inside. I made sure that I only got a little on Dan. I wanted him to be alive when the tank blew.

Tom turned the knob on the tank while opening the valve. The balloon slowly started to fill and Dan was back to pleading with me. I don't know what he said; I did not care to hear anything he said. As I was about to light my zippo and toss it on the passenger seat, Tom yelled at me again. He was letting me know to get away from the truck once I put the lighter in.

In hindsight, I can see how good that advice was. When I got to Tom's truck, the tank of ethylene had exploded. The booming sound had to be heard for some ways. It did not slow down a car on its way back to us. I could see the headlights of another vehicle coming back. I hurried up and got into Tom's truck. Without a word, he drove through some bushes, then followed a grassy path along a field to another country road with his lights off.

That was that. No more country life, no more of anything I knew. I sat there quietly till we got on the turnpike. Then I broke down and asked the one question on my mind. "Tom, What did I interview for?"

His response was not what I expected. He told me his name was not Tom, but his general code name is Stone and that is what everyone at the company knows him as. He told me to no longer call him Tom, but call him Stone. If I pass the next step, I would be working with him. He told me we were on our way to meet with his boss at Republic. By the time he finished telling me about Republic, we had left Ohio.

Seeing the sign that said welcome to Pennsylvania, I could only think how Scott Bearman was dead. I needed to figure out who Nathaniel Norris would be and what kind of work Stone would have me do. A phrase that I once heard came to my mind as I watched the trees pass.

Give up the past, glance at the future, but remember the present is where everything is done.

About The Author

E. A. Maynard had spent more years than he cares to count traveling the United States of America and has met many people that have guided him through great adventures. The good and bad is what he draws from in his writing. His adventures all began in Ohio. In fact, Ohio was where he lived for over thirty years until he moved to the Washington DC area. Now he lives in Virginia outside of D.C. and that is where home is now.

E. A. Maynard grew up in a small farm town in Northwest Ohio called Risingsun. It was a typical, small town when he was growing up. He was far from a saint, but when there is not much for a kid or teenager to do, they will find something to do. This led him to being very mischievous and took that well into being an adult. He also liked having fun, which lead to his mischievous nature.

E. A. Maynard has become much more laid back and now lives a different kind of adventure. He is a husband and a father. His family has been a strong theme in his past and present, so you will see this in his writing.

You can find more from E. A. Maynard at www.eamaynard.com and join the newsletter for updates.